Welcome to a month of fantastic reading, brought to you by Harlequin Presents! Continuing our magnificent series THE ROYAL HOUSE OF NIROLI is Melanie Milburne with *Surgeon Prince, Ordinary Wife*. With the first heir excluded from the throne of Niroli, missing prince and brilliant surgeon Dr. Alex Hunter is torn between duty and his passion for a woman who can never be his queen.... Don't miss out!

Also for your reading pleasure is the first book of Sandra Marton's new THE BILLIONAIRES' BRIDES trilogy, *The Italian Prince's Pregnant Bride*, where Prince Nicolo Barbieri acquires Aimee Black, who, it seems, is pregnant with Nicolo's baby! Then favorite author Lynne Graham brings you a gorgeous Greek in *The Petrakos Bride*, where Maddie comes face-to-face again with her tycoon idol....

In *His Private Mistress* by Chantelle Shaw, Italian racing driver Rafael is determined to make Eden his mistress once more...while in *One-Night Baby* by Susan Stephens, another Italian knows nothing of the secret Kate is hiding from their one night together. If a sheikh is what gets your heart thumping, Annie West brings you *For the Sheikh's Pleasure*, where Sheikh Arik is determined to get Rosalie to open up to receive the loving that only *he* can give her! In *The Brazilian's Blackmail Bargain* by Abby Green, Caleb makes Maggie an offer she just can't refuse. And finally Lindsay Armstrong's *The Rich Man's Virgin* tells the story of a fiercely independent woman who finds she's pregnant by a powerful millionaire. Look out for more brilliant books next month!

Harlequin Presents®

GREEK
TYCOONS

They're the men who have everything—
except brides...

Wealth, power, charm—
what else could a heart-stoppingly handsome
tycoon need? In THE GREEK TYCOONS
miniseries you have already been introduced to
some gorgeous Greek multimillionaires who are
in need of wives.

Now it's the turn of beloved Presents author
Lynne Graham, with her thrilling new romance
The Petrakos Bride

This tycoon has met his match, and he's decided
he *has* to have her...*whatever* that takes!

Lynne Graham

THE PETRAKOS BRIDE

GREEK
TYCOONS

HARLEQUIN®

TORONTO • NEW YORK • LONDON
AMSTERDAM • PARIS • SYDNEY • HAMBURG
STOCKHOLM • ATHENS • TOKYO • MILAN • MADRID
PRAGUE • WARSAW • BUDAPEST • AUCKLAND

ISBN-13: 978-0-373-12653-8
ISBN-10:   0-373-12653-0

THE PETRAKOS BRIDE

First North American Publication 2007.

All about the author…
Lynne Graham

Of Irish/Scottish parentage, LYNNE GRAHAM has lived in Northern Ireland all her life. She has one brother. She grew up in a seaside village and now lives in a country house surrounded by a woodland garden, which is wonderfully private.

Lynne first met her husband when she was fourteen. They married after she completed a degree at Edinburgh University. Lynne wrote her first book at fifteen, and it was rejected everywhere. She started writing again when she was home with her first child. It took several attempts before she sold her first book, and the delight of seeing that book for sale in the local newsagents has never been forgotten.

Lynne always wanted a large family, and she has five children. Her eldest, and her only natural child, is in her twenties and is a university graduate. Her other children, who are every bit as dear to her heart, are adopted: two from Sri Lanka and two from Guatemala. In Lynne's home, there is a rich and diverse cultural mix, which adds a whole extra dimension of interest and discovery to family life.

The family has two pets. Thomas, a very large and affectionate black cat, bosses the dog and hunts rabbits. The dog is Daisy, an adorable but not very bright West Highland white terrier, who loves being chased by the cat. At night, dog and cat sleep together in front of the kitchen stove.

Lynne loves gardening and cooking, collects everything from old toys to rock specimens and is crazy about every aspect of Christmas.

PROLOGUE

SURROUNDED by fawning celebrity guests and reverential relations at his engagement party, Giannis Petrakos felt as claustrophobic as a lion in a circus ring. His great-grandmother was beckoning him. The old lady was famous for her forthright opinions, and he guessed that she was eager to tell him what she thought of his fiancée. Grim amusement assailed Giannis; as one of the richest men in the world, he had learned to prize the sheer rarity value of such honesty.

Tiny in stature, Dorkas Petrakos settled snapping black eyes on her darkly handsome great-grandson as he towered over her. 'Krista is a very beautiful young woman. Every man here envies you.'

Giannis inclined his arrogant dark head in acknowledgement of the obvious, and waited for the axe to fall.

'But what sort of mother will she make for your children?' Dorkas enquired.

Giannis almost winced, for neither he nor Krista was ready to settle down to *that* extent. It had never occurred to him to consider his fiancée in the light of her maternal instincts. Perhaps in a few years they would have a child. But if that did not happen Giannis was prepared to choose a suitable successor to inherit his power and fortune from his extensive array of relatives. When it came to reproduction he had not a sentimental bone in his body.

'You think that doesn't matter. You think I'm out of date and out of touch,' the old lady opined, with a hint of aggression. 'But Krista is vain and selfish.'

His stubborn jawline tensed; such strong censure of his chosen bride was unwelcome. It struck him as unfortunate that just at that moment Krista should once again be visibly revelling in being the centre of attention. His fiancée could not pass a mirror or a camera without striking a pose. Blessed with turquoise eyes and white-blonde hair, Krista, with her stunning beauty, had attracted notice from the instant that she'd strolled into the public eye as a teenager. Heiress to the Spyridou electronics empire, and the only child of doting parents, Krista had been indulged from birth. How could his great-grandmother possibly understand her?

No two women could have had less in common. Born the daughter of a fisherman, Dorkas had grown up in grinding poverty and had held fast to her unpretentious values. Her refusal to conform to the ever more snobbish standards of her descendants and her blunt tongue had ensured that she was widely regarded by them as a social embarrassment. But there had always been a special bond between Dorkas and Giannis, formed most unexpectedly when he'd been a wildly rebellious teenager bent on self-destruction.

'You say nothing. But if you lost all your money and your fine houses and cars and aeroplanes tomorrow, would Krista still be by your side?' the old lady asked him drily. 'I think she'd run so fast you couldn't catch her!'

As he rose to leave his great-grandmother Giannis almost

laughed out loud, for in such a scenario Krista would only be a burden, awash with self-pity and recrimination. She was, undeniably, the product of her rarefied luxury environment. Did Dorkas truly believe that it was possible for him to find a woman impervious to the draw of his fabulous wealth? But the implication that Krista, however affluent in her own right, had an eye to the main chance touched his ego like the sting of a tiny needle sliding below the skin.

With a nod to his security chief, Nemos, to protect his privacy, Giannis strolled out on to the roof terrace. He enjoyed the fresh air while he questioned the bleak edge that had overtaken his mood. After all, he had no doubts about marrying Krista Spyridou. How could he have? Everyone regarded her as the perfect match for him. She had a classy pedigree and she was a terrific hostess. They belonged to the same exclusive world and she understood the rules. No matter what happened there would not be a divorce. In that way the Petrakos power-base of wealth and influence would be protected for another generation.

Yet Giannis did not forget that at nineteen years old, to the horror of his family and hers, he had dated Krista Spyridou and dumped her. The most beautiful girl in the world, he had discovered, seemed to have little else to offer. Indeed, he had decided that she was as cold as charity in bed—and out of it.

'*Please* don't wreck my hair…' That had been a favourite refrain.

'I really, *really* need my beauty sleep…'

'If you *must*…'

'I *hate* getting sweaty…'

Krista would never set his bedsheets on fire with enthusiasm, Giannis reflected wryly. Her lack of passion had been a deal-breaker when he was an idealistic teenager, powered by Dorkas's assurance that his perfect woman was out there, just waiting for him to find her. Well, nobody could say he hadn't looked. In fact, Giannis had packed in more than a decade of riotous womanising before reaching certain cynical and unapologetically selfish conclusions: his perfect woman did not exist. Also, he now saw Krista's flaws as positives that would ensure his marriage made the minimum possible impact on his lifestyle.

He was used to doing exactly as he liked when he liked. Marriage to Krista wouldn't change that; she would not cling or inflict unreasonable expectations on him, nor would she throw screaming tantrums demanding attention, love or fidelity. She would never care enough to do so. And what better wife could be found for a workaholic male who thrived on the high-powered pressure of business than a wife happy for him to keep his sexual options open? Krista would be much too busy pampering and clothing her perfect body to feel neglected by her billionaire husband.

As soon as Giannis rejoined the party Krista sped to his side, to beg him to share another photo opportunity. Not an ounce of his impatience showed on his lean, aristocratic face. Although he detested publicity, he was prepared to allow her her way at their engagement celebration.

Relieved by his lack of objection, Krista tucked a hand over his arm and became chatty. 'Is that horrid old crone in the corner from your tribe or mine?' she asked with a giggle.

Giannis glanced across the exquisitely furnished room and his eyes stilled on the little old lady dressed in unrelieved black and sitting erect. *Horrid old crone?* As Dorkas seldom left the island of Libos she was rarely recognised outside the family circle. His brilliant but semi-veiled dark eyes flashed smouldering gold.

'Why?'

'She actually asked me if I could cook. *Hello!*' Krista rolled her eyes with the supreme scorn of a young woman accustomed to being waited on hand and foot. 'Then she asked if I would be waiting for you when you got back from the office! *As if...*' she mocked. 'Someone should've left that old biddy at home. She embarrassed me. I do hope she won't be at our wedding.'

'If she isn't, I won't be either.' His response was smooth as silk.

Giannis watched his fiancée take a few seconds to comprehend what he was telling her. Shaken, Krista gave him an appalled look. Her long manicured nails dug into his sleeve in a panic before he could walk away. 'Giannis, I—'

'That old lady is my great-grandmother, and worthy of your deepest respect,' Giannis delivered with cold emphasis.

Aghast at having offended him, Krista grovelled. To the list of her flaws he added the sins of vulgarity and insincerity.

CHAPTER ONE

IN THE best of moods, and ready for her second day temping at Petrakos Industries, Maddie bounced on to the bathroom scales and stilled to look hopefully down at the gauge. She winced at the reading. Possibly it hadn't been a good idea to *jump* on them. She got off again. Shedding her nightdress and her watch, she reset the weighing machine and stepped on as lightly as possible. Disappointingly, the weight was identical.

'You can't keep body and soul together on that salad stuff,' old Mrs Evans who lived on the ground floor had opined, when Maddie had joined her and her daughter for a delicious three-course Sunday lunch, complete with all the trimmings, just a couple of days earlier.

Perhaps the 'salad stuff' would have been safer? Or possibly the bar of chocolate she had eaten on the way home from the supermarket the night before had been an over-indulgence too far? Could extra weight go on that fast? In truth, the long hours she worked just to pay the rent raised her healthy appetite to starvation proportions, and she still did not earn enough to eat well. Her despondent green eyes travelled across the expanse of her full-breasted, generous-hipped reflection. Generous mouth tightening, she looped impatient fingers through her torrent of long red hair, then anchored it back with a clip and got dressed at speed.

The black jeans and white blouse had a closer fit than she liked over her opulent curves, and she frowned. When a fire had broken out at her last address she had lost almost everything she possessed. Although she was trying to build up a new wardrobe by buying from charity shops, it wasn't easy on a low income. As she turned away from the mirror her attention fell on the photo of her late sister by her bed, and she scolded herself for being so precious about her appearance when she was lucky to have her health.

'Look on the bright side,' had been her grandmother's most constant refrain while she was growing up.

'Every cloud has a silver lining,' her grandfather had often chipped in with determination.

Yet Maddie and her grandparents had known a lot of heartbreak in their lives. Suzy, Maddie's beloved twin, had been diagnosed with leukaemia soon after the girls' eighth birthday. The stress of coping with Suzy's illness had destroyed their parents' marriage. Their paternal grandparents had taken charge, supporting Suzy through her gruelling treatment, her period of remission, and finally the last stages of her life. And ultimately it had been Suzy's fierce determination to get the most out of the time she'd had left that had taught Maddie the importance of hanging on to a cheerful outlook.

As she waited at the bus stop Maddie was struggling to subdue a juvenile tingle of excitement while she wondered if this would be the day she caught a glimpse of the legendary Giannis Petrakos again. Honestly, when she thought about him she felt more like a schoolgirl than a twenty-three-year-old grown-up! It was embarrassing to recall that she had once cherished a newspaper photo of the startlingly handsome Greek shipping tycoon. But she had been a teenager, and she'd developed a hopeless crush on him.

Petrakos Industries was a towering contemporary office block in the City of London. Maddie had never worked anywhere quite so imposing before, and the standards demanded of the staff were equally high. Even though she was only a temp, and generally entrusted with only menial tasks, her lack of qualifications had produced frowns on her first day. As always, she tried to compensate by being very hard-working and enthusiastic. She would have done just about anything to get a permanent job with such a company, because a decent salary would make a big difference to her life.

'Another five hundred jobs are being moved to Eastern Europe to cut costs,' a female voice lamented outside the room where Maddie was engaged in inputting onto a computer database. 'The press will go mental over it—'

'Petrakos Industries is in the top three most successful companies in the world,' male tones chipped in reprovingly. 'Giannis Petrakos may be a ruthless bastard, but he's invincible in business. Don't forget that his shark-like instincts are likely to deliver us an even bigger bonus this year.'

'Do you ever think about anything other than money?' the woman censured. 'Petrakos is a super-wealthy guy with about as much human emotion as a piece of granite.'

Maddie was tempted to go to the door and protest that point. But in her guise as an unwilling eavesdropper she knew she could scarcely do so. What was more, while she might long to sing Giannis Petrakos's praises, it was certainly not her place to talk about his private endeavours. Suppressing a sigh, she returned her attention to the database.

After lunch she and her agency co-worker, Stacy, were sent to the top floor to help out. A brunette manager called Annabel told Stacy that she would be serving refreshments at an afternoon meeting.

'I'm a temp, not a waitress!' Stacy declared pugnaciously.

'Your role as a temp is to do as you are asked,' Annabel retorted crisply. 'Petrakos Industries requires a high degree of flexibility from all employees—'

'I'm not an employee…I'm a temp—and I don't serve the tea—'

'Not to worry,' Maddie slotted in hastily, keen to bring the battle to an end before Stacy argued both of them out of a job. 'I'll do it.'

In receipt of that offer, Annabel defrosted only marginally, and angled a pointed look of disapproval at Maddie's jeans. 'The company dress code doesn't allow jeans, but I suppose you'll have to do.'

'You should've slapped that madam down hard for being so cheeky about your clothes,' Stacy opined the minute the two girls were alone. 'You're doing her a favour.'

Maddie grimaced. 'It was a fair comment. But with my skirt in the wash I only have jeans left to wear.'

'I bet she's just jealous of your looks,' Stacy contended with scorn. 'Those men walking out of the lift couldn't take their eyes off you, and she didn't like it.'

Maddie went red with embarrassment. 'I think she was just uptight about the meeting.'

'You should make the most out of what you've got,' Stacy told her impatiently. 'With your face and body, I'd be coining it in as a glamour model or a lap dancer.'

Inwardly cringing at the concept of that amount of naked

exposure, Maddie said nothing. Sometimes she thought she had been born into the wrong body, for she was very uncomfortable with the masculine notice awakened by her hourglass curves.

As she crouched down to remove a china tea-set from the cupboard where it was stored, Annabel thrust wide the door to issue further instructions. 'Mr Petrakos will be present at the meeting. When you enter the boardroom, serve the refreshments quietly and quickly.'

Striding past in advance of his personal staff, Giannis caught a glimpse of the redhead just before the boardroom kitchen door flipped shut on her. In that split second a razor-sharp image of her imprinted itself on his brain: bright hair that gleamed like beaten copper and gold against her pale alabaster skin and fell in splendour halfway down her spine; the luscious pout of voluptuous breasts that segued down into an improbably tiny waist and then flared out again into the ripe fullness of a very feminine derrière.

A powerful wave of testosterone-charged response assailed Giannis. He always controlled his sexuality, and he was startled by the heady rush of blood to his groin. He assumed his response was a rude reminder of a private truth: he liked women with a little more flesh than the very slender models who invariably came his way. Even so, that disruptive surge of sexual arousal irritated him, and he banished the image of her from his mind. Most probably, he acknowledged, he just needed a woman.

Taut with nerves at the prospect of finally seeing Giannis Petrakos again, Maddie immediately doubled up the amount of coffee in the flask she was preparing. Very strong and very sweet: that was how *he* liked it. For just a moment memories took over and she smiled, but she blinked back the tears that were pricking at the back of her eyes.

Under cover of the spirited dialogue taking place round the vast conference table, she eased the trolley into the boardroom and gently closed the door. Only then did she allow herself to look in the direction of the male poised by the windows, and even though she had promised herself that she would simply steal one tiny glance, she was transfixed. In the tailored perfection of a black pinstripe business suit, he looked downright magnificent.

If anything, Maddie conceded rather dizzily, he was even more staggeringly beautiful than when she had first seen him. Nine years had eradicated all trace of the boy from his lean strong face, and his powerful muscular frame had filled out. But he still held his proud dark head at an imperious angle that she instantly recognized, and his eyes were unforgettable. As dark as bitter aloes and set deep below straight ebony brows. His gaze was coolly trained on the current speaker. He had incredible eyes: in certain lights or when he laughed they were the same colour as gilded bronze.

'Why aren't you serving?' someone hissed in her ear.

Maddie unfroze, and jerked as though she had been slapped. As she reached for the first cup and saucer Giannis Petrakos glanced at her, and she stilled again. Her tummy flipped and her heart began to thump, making it hard for her to breathe. For the space of a heartbeat her surroundings vanished. All she was conscious of was the unfamiliar heaviness of her breasts, the dryness of her mouth, and the almost painful little twist of sensation making its presence felt low in her pelvis. She lowered her lashes in an instant of genuine confusion. It shook her that it took an almost physical effort to force her attention back to her task.

Coffee—strong, black, sweet, she reminded herself, while she wondered what on earth had come over her. And then, guessing, she felt a giant wave of shamed pink colour spreading up from her throat all the way over her dismayed face to her hairline. My goodness, she would never dare to look at him again! Dragging in a jerky breath, she poured his coffee, almost absentmindedly added four heaped spoonfuls of sugar, stirred it, and forced her feet in his direction.

Giannis had been bored, but now his ennui had fled. Had he not seen her again, he was sure he would not have thought of her. But her presence a scant twenty feet away put paid to that possibility. In a fluid movement he sat down at the table. Was she a private caterer? Or a member of the caterer's staff? Looking at her, he speedily lost interest in the finer details of her identity. Although she was decidedly pocket-sized in the height department, she had a gorgeous face, and the lushness of her full pink lips was a fitting match for the striking symmetry of her abundant curves. Her eyes were the colour of the green glass he had collected as a kid from the seashore. His shapely mouth curled as he recalled his exquisite mother's ridicule at receiving such a childish gift, but when he read the tiny curvaceous redhead's reverent gaze that unpleasant recollection of his disturbing childhood totally vanished.

Maddie set down his coffee with a hand that was shaking so badly he put out his own to steady her wrist and ensure there was not an accident.

'Be careful,' Giannis admonished.

It was only necessary to maintain the contact for seconds, but it was long enough for the faint floral scent of her fair skin to flare his nostrils. And that fast he got hot and hard again. In the startled quick upward glance she gave him he registered just how vulnerable she was. So close to him, she scarcely dared to breathe, and he found that knowledge incredibly exciting. He imagined tugging her down on to his lap, opening the shirt stretched to capacity over her ripe breasts and using his mouth and his hands to toy with the prominent crests that made faint indentations through the fine cotton. The strength of that erotic imagery surprised him, and he suppressed the fantasy with fierce disdain. Since when had he hit on the equivalent of a tea lady? He took a sip of the strong sweet brew in his cup, but the tension in his aroused body stubbornly refused to subside.

Warm all over, and trembling, Maddie backed away. What a clown she felt! What must he think of her for staring at him like that? Naturally he had noticed her gaping at him like a silly schoolgirl. How could he not have? He had braced her wrist with his fingers when he saw the cup wobbling on the saucer and told her off. A sidewise glance reassured her that nobody else appeared to have noticed his intervention, or his reproof. Relieved, but mortified by the poor showing she had made, she mustered her wits and hurried to serve the rest of the table.

'This coffee is undrinkable,' a man complained with a grimace, and was speedily backed up by his neighbour.

Consternation assailed Maddie.

'On the contrary—it's the first decent coffee I've had in this office,' Giannis said in an impatient tone of dismissal. 'Let's get on with the presentation.'

More flustered than ever by the critical comments, Maddie was quick to respond to a harried signal from Annabel Holmes that urged her to speed up the delivery of refreshments. In her eagerness to do that, and to contrive an escape from the conference room, Maddie caught her foot on an exposed wire. Stumbling, she pitched forward on to the carpet, and the laptop computer that had been jerked off the table when she tripped crashed down with her.

For split second there was total silence. Giannis studied the prone redhead with sardonic disbelief. She looked like an exquisite work of art but, being human, she had a fatal flaw: on the move, she was an accident waiting to happen.

'Why didn't you look where you were going?' one of the executives demanded in a tone of anguish.

'I'm so sorry,' Maddie gasped, staring in dismay at the computer.

'The USB memory stick has broken in half,' the man groaned, crouching down to assess the damage. 'I'll have to get another copy of the presentation e-mailed over, sir.'

Raw impatience filled Giannis, because he was on a very tight schedule. Not content with almost scalding him with the coffee, the redhead had just single-handedly wrecked the entire meeting. 'How could you be so incredibly clumsy?' he murmured in icy wonderment.

Horrified by the damage she had caused, and devastated by that personal rebuke, Maddie scrambled hurriedly upright and said tautly, 'I really am sorry, sir. I didn't see the wire.'

At that moment Giannis wondered what it was about her pale, delicate features that struck an eerie chord of familiarity with him. Whatever—a hint of tears had given her green eyes a soft radiance. An identification tag dangled from her shirt, but Giannis couldn't read it. He studied her from below the black screen of his dense lashes, his brilliant dark eyes glittering. Her pouting mouth reminded him of a crushed strawberry. 'And you are…?' he queried drily.

'Maddie…er…Madeleine Conway, sir.' Catching an urgent, dismissive jerk of the head from Annabel, who clearly wanted her to get out, and fast, she retreated back to the trolley and made a hasty exit.

Maddie felt so hot and flustered and furious with herself that she had to splash her face with cold water to cool down. Having actually got to meet Giannis Petrakos, she had contrived to make the worst possible impression on him. Her nerves had made her inexcusably ham-fisted. She winced at the suspicion that he might have seen the involuntary tears of dismay that had briefly filled her eyes when she'd realised the extent of the damage she had caused. How professional was that?

She felt even more uncomfortable about the way she had behaved around him. Being a touch naïve and inexperienced when it came to men now struck her as being a hanging offence. However, she had had little opportunity to be anything else when, from her teenage years right through to her early twenties, she had been restricted by her responsibilities at home. A social life had been impossible, school-friends had fallen away because she had never been free to go out. Though in some ways she had grown up older than her years, because she had spent so much time with her grandparents, when she'd moved to London to find work, after her grandmother had passed away, she had discovered that she was uncomfortably out of step with her peers. Sex as casual as a takeaway meal and heavy drinking ran contrary to the mores she had been taught to respect.

But Maddie was also honest enough to admit that until the moment she had looked across that conference room and seen Giannis Petrakos she had genuinely not known what it was to be strongly attracted to a man. In that instant her brain had turned to mush and her body to an alien entity that reacted with responses she had not known she had. The strength of that physical pull had taken her by surprise, and even in retrospect it shocked her. That disturbing awareness of the more private parts of her body still lingered like a secret taunt, to remind her that she had sexual responses that paid little heed to common sense or self-control. Could he have guessed why she was staring at him? The suspicion made her cringe. While he had to be accustomed to attracting female attention, he was entitled to expect more prudent behaviour from an employee.

'Miss Conway?' Annabel Holmes murmured from the doorway. 'A word, if you please.'

Maddie paled and turned obediently away from the trolley she had been clearing to face the manager.

'Are you sure you're all right? That was quite a fall you had,' the other woman remarked rather stiffly.

'I'm great—only my dignity dented,' Maddie asserted awkwardly. 'Were you able to hold the presentation?'

'I'm afraid not. There was a delay, and Mr Petrakos had another appointment. He's never here for long, and when he is his schedule is packed. Mistakes are an inconvenience and an annoyance that he doesn't forget,' Annabel breathed tautly. 'I messed up by asking you to do the refreshments—'

'No, I'm the one who messed up!' Maddie protested in dismay.

'I'm afraid Mr Petrakos has a low tolerance threshold for

screw-ups. I'm pretty sure I'll be forever associated with that ruined presentation in his mind.'

Guilt assailed Maddie in an even more powerful wave. 'Surely not… I mean, I'm sure he's a reasonable guy.'

A humourless laugh fell from Annabel's lips. 'You're suffering from the Petrakos effect, aren't you? All our hearts beat a lot faster the first time or so, but now mine just goes into panic mode when he's around,' she confided heavily. 'He may be drop-dead gorgeous, but he's cold as ice below the surface and he expects perfection. If you don't shape up, he ships you out fast.'

Initially ready to argue with that hard assessment of Giannis Petrakos, Maddie bit down on her tongue—because she had already learned for herself that he did not suffer fools in silence. She apologised again, for she could see that the brunette was sincerely worried about her future employment prospects.

Annabel shrugged and told her not to worry about it. 'That's the joy of being a temp,' the other woman added. 'You'll be out of here tomorrow and starting a clean sheet someplace else the next day.'

With a heavy heart, Maddie cleared the abandoned cups from the empty conference room. Surely Annabel Holmes was wrong about Giannis Petrakos, and was overreacting to an unfortunate blunder? But some highly successful business magnates *were* reputed to be total slave-driving tyrants in the office, Maddie acknowledged unhappily. And what did she really know about Giannis Petrakos as an employer? *Was* the other woman's career likely to suffer as a result of Maddie's clumsiness? If that was the case, wasn't it her duty to speak up on Annabel's behalf and ensure that she herself took the blame? Grovel in the hope that his memory of the unfortunate incident was forever associated with a very clumsy temp instead?

Tomorrow she would make every possible effort to speak to him. Perhaps when he arrived in the morning—or later—she'd be able to just manage to catch him on his own for a moment. She could always make him a cup of coffee and use that as an excuse to interrupt him. A couple of minutes would be all she needed. It was wonderful how a few well-chosen tactful words could smooth over an awkward episode…

CHAPTER TWO

GIANNIS woke hot and aching from an erotic dream and cursed with rare savagery. Maddie, the graceless little redhead, had hotwired his libido. What was it about her? The lure of forbidden fruit? The prospect of sex at the office? He had never had it, but had often thought about it.

Over the past decade he could have fulfilled that fantasy time and time again. Yet, in spite of the fact that innumerable female staff had made sexual approaches, he had never responded. He had withstood the ones who'd stripped off just as easily as he had rejected the looks, and the verbal and written invitations. In fact all those workplace come-ons had exasperated him, because he was first and foremost a businessman. He was a firm believer in enforcing the rules that kept his staff keen, disciplined, and motivated to deliver only their very best. By no stretch of the imagination could his shagging the temp do anything but damage that streamlined operational efficiency, Giannis told himself grimly.

On the other hand, he mused over breakfast at six, there was no reason why he should not pursue the temp once she had moved on from Petrakos Industries.

In the act of mulling over that fact, and its possibilities, on his chauffeur-driven journey through the London traffic, Giannis got a distinct cold chill down his spine. Why was he thinking about Maddie Conway so much? Why did he even remember her name? It was weird. He was acting weird. Since when had sex been a big deal to him? All his needs in that department were met by two highly sophisticated beauties, one in London and another in Greece. Both understood his requirements to the letter, and met them with the utmost style and discretion.

He set up a meeting over lunch with his English mistress. Obviously he was suffering from sexual frustration.

At noon, Maddie felt a yawn creeping up on her. She had been given a heap of photocopying to do, and it was so tedious that she could have fallen asleep standing up. Stacy's moans made the chore no more enjoyable.

'We always get the jobs nobody else wants to do,' Stacy complained bitterly. 'Filing or running messages.'

'I'm not qualified to do much else,' Maddie responded

'I honestly think that uppity cow Annabel sat down last night to work out a list of boring stuff to land us with.' Stacy restocked the photocopier with paper in a series of vicious movements.

Maddie lifted her head as she heard steps on the stairs outside the door. 'She's really okay…' Her voice lost strength and ebbed without her awareness when she focused on the male coming to a halt just outside the door.

Lowering the mobile phone from his ear, Giannis Petrakos glanced casually into the room on his way past, and then came to a momentary halt.

'Is there anyone you *don't* like?' Stacy was demanding in

a tone of irritation, her back turned to the door. 'It's not normal to always be saying nice things about everybody.'

Maddie parted her lips to laugh off that response, but no sound came out—because incisive dark, deep-set eyes were surveying her from the doorway. She couldn't move, couldn't break that visual connection. A strange sense of exhilaration gripped her. Her heart was racing so fast it seemed to be pounding in her eardrums. Her skin prickled and tightened round her bones. And then he swung away and strode down the corridor, leaving her limp and drained and in shock again. For goodness' sake, what was wrong with her? He had only looked in her direction for a couple of seconds and she had stared back at him as if she was paralysed! Couldn't she have at least smiled and acted as if she had more than one brain cell?

She would have liked to tell him that she would never forget how happy he had made her sister, but her grandmother's gratitude at the time had made him uncomfortable, and not for worlds would she have repeated that mistake. In any case, she acknowledged ruefully, it was most unlikely that after so many years he would even remember her late sister.

'Hello? 'Stacy snapped her fingers loudly right in front of Maddie's face, to recapture her co-worker's attention. 'Anybody home?'

In his office, Giannis was engaged in the unfamiliar task of questioning his own actions. His lean, fiercely handsome features were taut with incomprehension. Emerging from the boardroom, he had shaken off his phalanx of support staff and had traversed the entire top floor of Petrakos Industries. He had looked into rooms he had not even known existed. Why? Why had he done that? For the first time in his life he had done something that he did not remember deciding to do, and he had done it for no good reason.

He was exasperated by the suspicion that he might have been prompted by a subconscious desire to see the red-headed temp again. And he was annoyed that her Titian red hair, smooth alabaster skin and full breasts had stood up so well to a second, more critical scrutiny. In fact, dressed in a simple white shirt and a narrow black skirt that could only showcase her dazzling curves, she had looked more ravishing than ever. That acknowledgement seriously rattled him.

He was on the way to his mistress's apartment when Krista called him.

'I've decided on an Ancient Greek theme for our wedding,' his fiancée trilled in high excitement. 'You said you wanted a traditional wedding. What could be more traditional than the ancient gods?'

'They were pagans,' Giannis said drily.

'Who cares about that? Piety is deeply unfashionable. Our wedding will be the society event of the year. You can play Zeus, the king of the gods, and I can be Aphrodite, the goddess of beauty—'

'According to Homer, Zeus and Aphrodite were father and daughter.' As Giannis had not the slightest intention of getting tricked out in a tunic and cloak to make a fashion statement out of what he considered to be a private and serious event, he hoped that nobody told her that Adonis had been one of Aphrodite's many lovers.

Fifteen minutes later, Giannis greeted his English mistress. Sex, he was convinced, would restore him to the cool rationality of his normal self. Over the past twenty-four hours he had become increasingly aware that he was not himself. Not a male given to solemn self-examination, he found himself furiously intolerant of his undisciplined thoughts, disturbed sleep and edgy behaviour.

Unfortunately, the instant he laid eyes on the beautiful blonde model he realised that he no longer found her attractive. All of a sudden, and for no reason that he could understand, she left him stone-cold. What was more, he found himself making an unwelcome comparison between her and Maddie Conway. For a male who functioned on pure logic, such perverse mental ruminations were deeply disturbing. Duly informed that their arrangement had run its course, the blonde accepted the news with good grace, since she was well aware that she would receive a generous financial settlement.

Giannis got back into his limo, having enjoyed neither the release of sexual tension nor the indulgence of an appetising lunch. Even his impatience felt unfamiliar, for his personal life, like his working day, was highly organised and designed to meet his every expectation. He liked the framework of his existence to be predictable. In his choice of Krista as a bride he had left nothing to chance, because he knew that she would never demand more than he was prepared to give. The sole surviving offspring of selfish and irresponsible parents, he took no risks in his private life. He satisfied his high sex drive with the minimum of fuss and emotion and, while he might specialise in the superficial in his relationships, he had never slept around.

In short, lusting after a sexy little red-headed temp at the office was decidedly not his style. She did not share his background or his place in society. She was not even his type—his usual preference was for leggy blondes. Yet her translucent ivory complexion, verdant green eyes and luscious pink mouth had become imprinted on his brain with the efficiency of a rampantly destructive computer virus, Giannis reflected in angry frustration. He was determined to repress such unruly promptings. It would be an act of crass stupidity to seek intimacy with an employee, however temporary. Even if she *had* looked at him with a wondering air of reverence that, he had to confess, he found stupendously appealing…

By late afternoon, Maddie appreciated that she had little time left in which to seek out Giannis Petrakos and say her piece about the laptop débâcle. In less than an hour she would be leaving the Petrakos building, and tomorrow she would be working someplace else. Having heard Stacy getting her instructions prior to taking over the switchboard, she knew that the Greek tycoon was in his office and that his calls were being diverted. She wasn't going to get a better chance to speak to him.

   Unfortunately, she was stopped during her passage upstairs and sent to pick up some papers from another floor. She had to wait until they were ready, and by the time she delivered them back there were only twenty minutes of her working day left. In the galley kitchen she hastily took out a cup and saucer and made coffee exactly the way Giannis Petrakos liked it.

   She moved down the corridor as fast as she dared. She no longer knew if he was even still in the office, and there was no time to find out. Her stomach felt as though it was lodged somewhere near her throat. Balancing the coffee in one hand, she knocked on the door of his office. There was no answer. Afraid that she would be noticed and intercepted before she could see him, she depressed the door handle with a perspiring palm.

   'Can I help you?' A man the size of a skyscraper had appeared out of nowhere and materialised at her elbow when she'd least expected it. His accent was foreign, his craggy dark face cold. She shot a nervous glance up at him, wondering who he was.

'I've made some coffee for Mr Petrakos. Who are you?'

'Nemos. I take care of Mr Petrakos's security.' The older man rested his attention on her name-tag, and then surprised her by pressing open the door for her entry. 'Go ahead, Miss Conway.'

The office of the CEO of Petrakos Industries was a vast space, with a strikingly contemporary décor, but it was frustratingly empty. At a loss, Maddie hovered until she heard a slight noise through an open door on the other side of the huge room.

A pulse beating suffocatingly fast in her throat, she went through that door and found herself in a connecting hallway. With a frown, she looked to right and left.

'Who is it?' a familiar accented drawl enquired with impatience.

Taut with concern at the suspicion that she might once again be acting as an irritation, Maddie turned to the left to answer his query. 'I've made you coffee, Mr Petrakos…'

One step through that door and Maddie appreciated her mistake, coming to a stricken halt as she realised she had entered some sort of dressing area lined with mirrored closets. Her dismayed gaze whipped over a unit on which a monogrammed silver clothesbrush had been abandoned She realised that a bathroom lay through the communicating door a mere instant before Giannis Petrakos himself strode into view, with his black hair still damp and spiky from the shower. His white shirt was hanging open to display a sleek muscular wedge of brown chest. His feet were bare beneath the hems of his immaculately tailored trousers. Obviously she had interrupted him while he was getting dressed.

'Oh…oh, my goodness. I'm so s-sorry!' Maddie stammered in intense mortification.

Taken aback by her appearance, because his bodyguards were highly efficient at protecting his privacy, Giannis surveyed her. He was astonished that she could have bypassed his security team. But, as appreciation of her beauty flamed through him and unleashed an instantaneous sexual response, his aggressive hunting instincts took over. He decided that only fate could have set up such an opportunity. After all, she had entered his private quarters without invitation, and they were alone where no one would dare to disturb him.

'I thought this was another office… I had no idea.' Too embarrassed to look directly at him, Maddie was engaged in swiftly backing out again. 'Please excuse my intrusion.'

'But you brought coffee? For me? ' Giannis treated her to a stunning smile and stretched out a lean brown hand to signify a welcome. 'How very kind.'

The megawatt impact of that unexpected smile curving his wide sculpted mouth dazzled Maddie. Her tummy executed a back-flip without warning, and all the oxygen in her lungs seemed to vanish. She would not let her attention dip below the level of his angular jaw. She knew she had stuff to say to him, but her memory had suddenly become one giant horrendous blank.

'Mr Petrakos…excuse me,' she managed breathlessly.

'No.' Giannis was studying her, and discovering that her emerald-green eyes had a breathtaking clarity. He found the contrast between her white skin and copper hair exotic and unusual. Every time he saw her he registered something new to savour.

'I beg your pardon?' Maddie was amazingly aware of the appraisal of those intense gilded bronze eyes. While it made her feel self-conscious, she very much liked that visual attention. In fact a whole host of alien sensations were striking her all at once. The most basic was that that lean dark countenance of his had a fatal fascination for her. She stared, and she couldn't help staring, taking in every individual feature with a fervour she couldn't deny. The sleek tawny planes of his high, hard cheekbones accentuated the dramatic dark brilliance of his gaze, while his arrogant nose and the rougher shadowed skin round his wilful passionate mouth lent a tough, masculine edge to a face at risk of being hauntingly beautiful.

'I said no—you are not excused,' Giannis extended lazily, as he eased the cup and saucer from her paralysed grip and set it down on a polished cabinet. 'I want you to stay and talk to me.'

'Talk?' Maddie echoed in confusion, striving valiantly to recover her concentration. 'Of course, you want to know what I'm doing in here—'

'Possibly I've already worked that one out,' Giannis murmured, with the husky amusement of a male accustomed to frequent feminine overtures.

Disconcerted by that reply, Maddie blinked and then coloured. 'I'm sure you appreciate that it was entirely my fault that the presentation couldn't be held. I wasn't looking where I was going—'

Giannis closed a hand over hers, unlacing her taut fingers and spreading them within the hold of his in a calming gesture. 'You're very nervous.'

Something like a flock of butterflies had broken loose in

Maddie's tummy. The warmth of his hand on hers, the smooth brush of his fingertips against the sensitive inner skin of her wrist, was making her tingle all over. While surprised by the ease with which he touched her, she was warmed by it as well. Even believing that he meant nothing by that minor intimacy, she found it a challenge to catch her breath. 'That's why I tripped yesterday—'

Uninterested in the topic she was striving to follow, and single-minded as always, Giannis shrugged back the cuff of his shirt to reveal his Swiss platinum watch. 'In ten minutes you will no longer be in my employ,' he spelt out. 'Do I have to wait that long to kiss you?'

Her green eyes opened to their widest extent. She was utterly silenced by that question.

'I would never trouble an employee with unwelcome attention,' Giannis completed softly.

With a handful of words, spoken with the utmost calm and cool, he had plunged her into shock. *Do I have to wait that long to kiss you?* He was telling her that he found her attractive, and she was astonished by that concept. He felt the same way she did? A sense of joy followed on that thought, and blew away her usual caution.

'Madeleine…?' Giannis prompted, registering his own level of ardour with a faint stab of unease.

Even the way he said her name sent a delicious frisson travelling down Maddie's taut spinal cord. She was so tense her muscles literally ached. 'It's…it's not unwelcome,' she heard herself tell him unevenly.

'I did not think it would be, *glikia mou.*'

Giannis approached her with the skill of a very experienced male, but beneath the surface he was aware of a pulse of desire that ran much hotter and stronger than he was accustomed to. Off-balance at that suspicion, he saw there was the faintest tremor in the long brown fingers he curved to her narrow shoulder to draw her to him. It was a struggle to master the fierce passion that prompted him to crush her hungrily to his lean, powerful frame. He liked the telling dilation of her pupils and the slight audible catch of breath in her throat when he lifted his hand to undo the clasp at the nape of her neck.

'My hair…' she said in surprise as he let the clasp fall. She scarcely knew what she was saying, for she was at such a height of expectation she could barely formulate a single thought, never mind a sensible sentence.

Giannis tugged the silky tangle of long hair round her triangular face, rejoicing in the freedom to do so. The sensual contrast between the wine-red strands and the pearlised perfection of her skin delighted him. 'It's magnificent…you should always wear it loose.'

'It would get in my way,' she muttered with a nervous laugh.

'But I want it to get in mine.' Giannis laced brown fingers into the bright strands and lowered his proud dark head.

Maddie could barely wait for him to kiss her, and her keenness embarrassed her. It did not seem quite nice for her to be so eager, but she couldn't help it. Deep in her pelvis there was a hard, tight knot of anticipation, and it was a challenge to keep her feet still. Heart racing inside her chest, and barely breathing, she leant almost imperceptibly forward.

When the tip of his tongue traced the full, sultry curve of her lips she shivered. He delved between with a dark, demanding eroticism that flamed through her slim body as efficiently as an arrow hitting a bullseye. Her head swimming, she fought to contain her response. Her slim fingers clenched in on themselves. Her body went rigid even while she was achingly conscious of the stinging heat pinching her nipples tight, of the scratchy and delicious awareness prickling over her entire skin surface. She wanted to grab him but she wouldn't let herself.

'I could devour you,' Giannis growled, his dark golden gaze ablaze as he laced one powerful hand into her tumbling copper hair to tug her head back.

Adrenalin was pounding through her veins like an electric charge. Meeting his eyes, she felt a kind of elation fill her, linked with the charged sense of readiness holding her fast. He buried his hungry, masculine mouth against the delicate skin of her throat, probing and nipping the tender spots with a sure and sensual skill that made her gasp. With his other hand he pressed her into closer connection with his lithe, rock-hard frame. By the time he claimed her ripe pink lips she was on fire for that kiss, craving it. The great wild whoosh of excitement engulfed her like a bonfire.

'You're amazing,' he told her thickly

'So are you…' Green eyes bright as stars, Maddie looked up at him, acknowledging the astounding sense of connection she was feeling. It made no sense, but it was there, and her every nerve-ending seemed to be jumping up and down and staging a celebration. She needed his support because she was dizzy, and her legs felt as weak and insubstantial as twigs. Momentarily she recalled the other men who had kissed her. She had never felt anything more than the mildest satisfaction, and more often than not it had been an endurance test in embarrassment.

'I knew you would be,' Giannis swore, bending down to push an arm below her hips and haul her up into his arms without any noticeable effort.

Maddie vented her astonishment in a gasp.

When he kissed her again she speared her fingers into his luxuriant black hair and opened her lips to the erotic plunge of his tongue. The world spun in a multi-coloured haze of excitement behind her lowered eyelids. She shivered violently, and his arms tightened round her before he brought her down on a cushioned surface. The surprise of that move made her lashes lift, and she focused in bewilderment on the unfamiliar room and on the bed upon which she lay. Uncertainty and a slight hint of panic made her tense.

Giannis rested fluid tanned fingers along her delicate jawbone to turn her attention to the compelling force of his dark golden gaze instead. 'I want you, *glikia mou.*'

'Yes…' Although that truth struck her as the most extraordinary thing since time began, she believed him absolutely, and it made her feel incredibly happy and blessed. The hunger etched in every angle of his lean, extravagantly handsome face thrilled her. It unlocked something inside her, blurred all ability to reason, and she acted on instinct when she stretched up and found his beautifully shaped mouth again for herself.

He raised her up and removed her shirt without her even having been aware that it had been unbuttoned. Before she could take fright he locked his urgent mouth to hers again, and unhooked her bra. Unremarked, the garment fell away. An almost inaudible moan was wrenched from low in her throat as the swollen buds of her distended nipples were grazed by the hair-roughened expanse of his hard, muscular chest. With a groan of satisfaction he curved his hands to the voluptuous creamy curves of her breasts.

'I love your body, *glikia mou,*' he growled against her reddened lips.

While she sucked in a panting breath, assailed by a sense of disbelief that such intimacy could possibly be taking place, he cupped the ripe, honey-soft swells and kneaded the lush rose-pink nipples already pouting for his attention. She quivered and gasped in helpless response, her breath rasping in her throat. A pulse of sweet, seductive pleasure began to beat at the heart of her. Such consuming sensuality had never touched her before, and she had no resistance whatsoever.

Giannis looked down into her lovely face with intense appreciation. He liked her lack of guile and affectation. She made sex so simple he was enthralled. Her bemusement, her unhidden surprise at what she was feeling, made him suspect that she might not be anything like as experienced as his usual partners. Unexpectedly he found that conviction the hottest turn-on he'd had in years. He kicked out the little voice at the back of his mind that suggested he should be more circumspect. He had not felt so fiercely aroused since he was a teenager. And she had come to him freely. What harm could there possibly be in taking his pleasure?

'You're so beautiful,' he told her huskily, easing her narrow skirt down below her hips, then casting it aside.

So are you, she longed to tell him, and her face warmed. She trembled, lost in her wondering admiration of him and yet incredibly shy as well. But he brushed her hand away when she made a sudden fumbling attempt to cover the brazen bareness of her breasts. Lest she had any thought of repeating that attempt, he lowered his tousled black head to skilfully entrap a pouting rosy crest between his lips. With a whisk of his tongue he teased the tormented peak to a rigid point of aching need.

Maddie didn't know what had hit her. Her spine arched up

off the bed. Her hips discovered a sinuous beat in tune with the swollen dampness between her legs. He sat up to discard his shirt, and in the midst of the exercise he kissed her fiercely. She was electrified by the erotic feel of his erection against her lower thigh. The barrier of his clothes could not conceal his bold masculine arousal.

'Feel what you have done to me,' he rasped, taking her hand and curving her fingers to the blatant bulge of his manhood. 'I ache for you…'

Surprise and excitement engulfed her as he pushed against her hand with an earthy need that shocked her. But it was a shock that she found insidiously attractive. 'Giannis…'

He reacted to the sound of his name on her lips by reaching for her again with a savage impatience that thrilled her. 'I can't resist you,' he groaned, pinning her half beneath him to plunder the luscious fullness of her mouth while he scooped up her knees and dexterously skimmed off her panties.

Maddie tensed, suddenly feeling wildly and dangerously naked and vulnerable. What was she doing? *What on earth was she doing?* A little voice screamed at the back of her head. She might have adored Giannis Petrakos on sight when she was fourteen—but did that mean that the first chance she got she went the whole way with him? Threw away the whole rule book and slept with him?

Long fingers flirted with the feathery Titian curls that covered her feminine mound and she froze, all thought and debate instantly suspended. Her entire body clenched taut with seething anticipation.

'Take it easy, *pedhi mou*,' Giannis urged raggedly, struggling to rein back a hunger that he still found unnervingly strong. But he had a stronger need to live up to the expectant wondering look he had seen in her gaze the day before.

He found the tantalising triangle between her thighs and she shivered helplessly, crazily aware of the tenderness of that secret place. So hot, so damp, so tense she almost physically hurt with longing. Her intense response made her jerk and squirm as he explored the swollen pink folds and stroked the tiny hidden bud, releasing a storm of sensation that made her cry out and gasp. An erotic flood of feeling sent her out of control and took her to the edge of a desperation she had not known existed.

'I can't stand it…' she framed, twisting her head back and forth on the pillow, barely knowing what she was saying while she was entrapped in this world of sensual torment.

Hotter than he had ever been for the ultimate completion, Giannis needed no second invitation. He slid with hard, fluid grace between her slender thighs. With an urgent groan of satisfaction his bold shaft forged a passage into her tight, honeyed channel. At the same instant as he plunged through the fragile barrier of her resisting flesh a startled whimper of pain was dragged from her. Bemused by that slight obstruction, he stilled, uncertain and incredulous, to stare down into her darkened green eyes in question.

'*Theos mou…*Madeleine—this cannot be.'

For an instant the real world intruded, and she recoiled from the thoughts threatening at the back of her mind. A dark pulse of voluptuous yearning was still pounding through her unbearably tense body. The simmering heat created by his passionate invasion was firing up again now that the initial discomfort had ebbed. He felt astonishing. She shut her eyes tight, told herself it was far too late to be worrying, and wrapped her arms round him in silent encouragement.

A shudder racked his lithe, powerful body and then he gave way, withdrawing from her only to surge back into her again in even more powerful possession. Excitement electrified her in a seductive wave, and she tilted up to him in sinuous welcome. Control fell away, shattered by the tight coil of pressure in her pelvis that made her crave him like a drug. He slammed back into her, hot and hard. She cried out in delight. Once begun, the delirious pleasure surged higher and higher, and time lost all meaning until finally she reached an explosive physical crescendo. Glorious waves of ecstasy racked her trembling body in ultimate release and she sank into a shell-shocked reverie.

Giannis stroked the vibrant coppery hair back from her smooth white brow. He pressed his mouth there very softly, and then wondered what he was playing at—because he had never been into all that fake, lovey-dovey cuddling stuff. Stung by that awareness, he lifted his handsome dark head again as if he had been burnt. The instant she shifted away from him, however, he automatically pinned her back beneath a hair-roughened powerful thigh. He wanted more of her. More and more and more, he acknowledged in a sensual daze of anticipation.

He had never had sex that amazing. Something that had become a rather boring routine, like a morning shower, had suddenly become full of exciting erotic possibilities again. She was a magnificent discovery. With subtle movements he shifted her across the mattress and covertly kicked aside the sheet so that he could examine it. There was a bloodstain on the linen. She *had* been a virgin. A one hundred per-cent-genuine virgin.

On one level he was sincerely shocked that he had taken

advantage of so inexperienced a girl. On another, he'd hit a total erotic high and felt very smug about the fact that she had surrendered her innocence to him. Not much given to point-less regrets, Giannis suppressed the rare guilt factor and revelled in the erotic high instead. He had found her, he had awakened her…she was all his. He decided not to comment. Why make a big deal of it if she didn't?

The phone by the bed lit up and vibrated. Giannis answered it. It was Nemos, reminding him that the jet was on standby for his flight to Berlin.

Listening to the swift exchange in Greek, Maddie was depth-charged out of her stasis and fully and fatally restored to awareness again. Consternation gripped her. She was gen-uinely appalled and confused by what she had allowed to happen between them. Raised by a grandmother who had taught her to believe that it was a woman's job to set the moral boundaries with a man, she immediately felt that most of the blame had to be hers.

Only as Giannis cast aside the phone did he register a reality that shook him out of his complacency. His ebony brows pleated in displeasure. 'The condom split.'

Sitting up, desperate to make an escape and already mea-suring the distance to the door, Maddie froze at that informa-tion. She had still to look anywhere near him.

'Are you using anything that might prevent conception?' Giannis enquired without expression, picturing the poten-tial impact of such a calamity and barely managing to repress a shudder.

In no fit state to deal with the risk of an accidental preg-nancy, Maddie had turned pale as parchment paper. It seemed to her that the punishments for her wanton misconduct were already piling up thick and fast, threatening to bury her alive. What was shame and humiliation in comparison to a life-changing event like conceiving a child?

'No,' she muttered tightly.

Giannis noticed that she was as far away from him as she could get and still be in the same bed. 'I'm sure we'll be okay. Accidents do happen, but there's no reason why this one should lead to a disaster.'

'I'm sure,' she agreed hastily, but her mortified sense of hurt had deepened. No, she didn't want to be pregnant either, but his response underscored her cringing belief that she had made the biggest ever fool of herself *and* acted like a slut. Naturally it would be a disaster if someone like her got into the family way because of someone like him. She reached down to snatch up her shirt, which was lying on the floor, and dug her arms jerkily into it. Her only thought was of flight.

'Madeleine—'

In frantic haste she was gathering up her discarded apparel, a glow of shamed pink illuminating her downbent face. 'There's nothing to talk about,' she muttered in apologetic interruption, eager to forestall the threatening intimacy of discussing anything with him and to make good her escape. 'I'll be totally fine.'

Unaccustomed to being interrupted, Giannis sprang out of bed just as Maddie vanished into the bathroom. The door closed. Elegant brows lifted in surprise, he heard the lock turn.

Behind the door, Maddie was engaged in the act of fever-ishly reclothing her shivering body. Her hands were all fingers and thumbs and her mind was throwing up distressing images and unwelcome realities. She had just gone to bed with a man she barely knew. And whose fault was that? She had made one mistake after another, right from the moment she had failed to conceal the fact that she found him incredibly attractive. Naturally he had registered that, and was it any wonder that he had got the wrong impression of her? When she'd had the effrontery to enter his inner sanctum with the offer of a coffee he hadn't asked for, he had interpreted her approach as an invitation. A sexual invitation, she conceded sickly. How could she have been so utterly stupid? An arrestingly handsome and wealthy male must often receive such physical advances—and what young, single guy said no to such an opportunity?

As silently as she could, she released the lock, opened the door and crept out.

Giannis collided with wide green eyes full of dismay, and registered that his continuing presence appeared to be unwelcome to her. As no woman had ever looked at him in that way, he assumed that the impression was misleading. 'I have a flight to catch.'

'Of course,' Maddie mumbled, striving to edge past him.

'We'll talk when I get back to London,' Giannis declared, even while knowing he had not the slightest intention of breaking his lifetime rule of never, ever discussing anything in the way of relationships with a woman.

'I—' Before she even knew what she planned to say, long brown fingers framed her flushed cheekbones.

His black hair still enticingly tousled by her clutching fingers, he bent his arrogant dark head and claimed a brief, devouring kiss that momentarily silenced her. 'I'll call you,' he told her with customary casualness.

'No…no, don't,' Maddie countered tightly, her lips tingling and her cheeks burning with colour. She was furious with herself for standing still and accepting that final kiss without so much as an attempt to turn her head away.

Halfway into the bathroom, Giannis paused, frowned, and turned his bold profile back to her, wondering if he had misunderstood.

'I know you must want to forget this happened,' Maddie added in an uneasy rush.

'Not in this case. I'll be in touch, *glikia mou.*' And with that indolent reply, Giannis dealt her a wolfish smile of amusement and headed back into the shower.

His confidence was unshakeable: women always responded to him with eager encouragement. She'd hardly been able to meet his eyes, but her soft mouth had surrendered beneath his in an indisputable response. Had she thought he needed an excuse *not* to see her again? He almost laughed out loud while he marvelled at her naivety. Possibly she was feeling a little overwhelmed by him, and the swift passage of events. She would get over that sensitive streak soon enough, he reflected with innate cynicism. With his input her ordinary life would, in the near future, change into something very much more stimulating. She would be the starring attraction in his bedroom for quite some time to come…

CHAPTER THREE

EMERGING from the CEO's office suite into the corridor, Maddie was relieved to discover that the majority of the staff had already gone home. At a fast trot she collected her bag and her jacket, and was about to get into the lift when she was intercepted by Nemos.

'Mr Petrakos asked me to ensure that you get home safely,' the Greek security man informed her. 'A car is waiting downstairs at the side entrance.'

Startled by his appearance, because in spite of his size he moved with remarkable stealth, Maddie was still more dismayed at the unexpected offer of a lift home. An agonised flush blossomed in a betraying burst of scarlet beneath her fair skin. She could not bear to think that anyone else might have guessed what she had so lately been engaged in.

'No, thank you,' she gasped in an agitated undertone, and, as Nemos gazed down at her in frank surprise, she hurriedly slid past him and into the lift before the doors could close again and leave her marooned.

Maddie didn't breathe again until she had left the building. She knew that she would never willingly set foot in Petrakos

Industries again. All the way home on the bus she was tormented by the aftermath of shock—regret and self-loathing.

What on earth had possessed her to behave in such a way? To give her body to a guy who was almost a stranger?

Yet Giannis hadn't felt like a stranger, and it seemed to her that foolish false sense of familiarity had stifled all her wit and common sense. She had behaved like a starstruck groupie, she thought painfully. Nine years had passed since she first laid wondering eyes on Giannis Petrakos. She had been just fourteen years old when he'd visited her sister Suzy in hospital. At the age of twenty-two, when—ironically—he'd been getting loads of bad press for being a wild and womanising hellraiser, he had been quietly giving considerable time and cash to the cause of terminally sick children.

Born though Giannis had been, into a world of unimaginable wealth and privilege, he had sat down to chat to Suzy as if it had been the most natural thing in the world. When he'd discovered that Suzy idolised the lead vocalist in a famous boy band, he had brought the singer to the hospice where Suzy had spent her final weeks. He'd made her sister's wildest dreams come true. Suzy had been so thrilled that she had still been talking about that momentous day right up until a few minutes before she died.

Maddie had never forgotten how happy Giannis Petrakos had made her twin. Now she recognised how she had idealised him and begun imagining that she knew him when she did not. She felt she had been too quick to seize on Annabel's concerns as an excuse to approach Giannis and talk to him alone. Why hadn't she immediately backed off when she'd realised that he was only semi-clothed? His apparent interest in her had gone to her head like strong spirits. She had not had the strength of will to withstand temptation. And he had been unutterably, wildly tempting. The dulled throb between her slender thighs lingered to remind her of her weakness and her sense of shame increased. Passion had made her betray her values.

Only as Maddie reached her bedsit did she remember the accident with the contraception, and her skin turned clammy with instinctive fear. She could only hope that Giannis would be proved right in his belief that there would be no repercussions in that field. She was appalled at the idea of conceiving after the equivalent of a one-night stand with a male who would regard the development as a calamity. Any child forced to deal with such wounding knowledge of its beginnings would have a right to be disgusted with her. How the mighty have fallen, she reflected, with painful new self-knowledge.

The days passed for Maddie at a painfully slow pace. She was restless, worried and unhappy. The sense of peace she had taken for granted had been replaced by inner turmoil. Nothing that she was feeling was quite what she felt it ought to be, either. Every time her phone sounded she jumped and snatched it up. Either it was a call from the temping agency or from the supermarket where she did weekend shifts. When she finally grasped the fact that she had been waiting to see if Giannis would phone, she was even angrier with herself. It was already painfully clear: she had been bedded and discarded as if she had no more worth than an old newspaper.

The following Saturday morning, however, someone rapped on her door. Looping her tumbling hair back from her face as she answered it, she stilled in astonishment when she recognised that her caller was Giannis's security chief.

'Mr Petrakos wants you to join him for lunch,' Nemos announced with precision. 'He'll pick you up in an hour.'

Her delicate brows pleating, Maddie stared up at the big man. It took her a few seconds to absorb that most unexpected message. Not so much a message as a royal summons, she registered, watching Nemos clatter back down the stairs again without even waiting for her response. Evidently there was a strong assumption that nobody *ever* said no to an invitation from Giannis Petrakos.

Maddie leant back against the door as she closed it. Her knees felt a little wobbly. A giant wave of incredulity was washing over her. He had ignored her existence for the rest of the week and now he was issuing a last-minute offer of a lunch-date on a take-it-or-leave-it basis. Naturally she would be leaving it. For a tiny, tiny fraction of a split second she had felt a leap of joy that he had not totally forgotten her existence, but she swiftly crushed that shameful reaction. Where did he get the nerve to act as if she was some servant at his beck and call?

You gave him the nerve, a little inner voice jibed. He hadn't even had to ask her out to get her into bed. She had been a push-over—a sure thing. Evidently he expected her to drop everything and run the instant he chose to beckon. And why not? She had set no limits and demanded no respect that day at his office. It hurt her to acknowledge it, but she had behaved like a slut. Now he was treating her with a careless, casual indifference to her feelings that could only wound her even more.

Inwardly cringing at the hard lesson she felt she was being taught, she got changed for her shift at the supermarket. Slowly and surely, however, anger was starting to lace her turbulent feelings.

When a knock sounded on the door again, Maddie was

ready for it. Before Nemos could even speak, she said tightly, 'I'm not coming. I don't want to see your employer again. It's up to you how you tell him that.'

Disbelief followed by consternation flickered in the older man's craggy features before he turned on his heel. The depth of her anger dismayed Maddie, for she had always believed that she had the most placid, even-tempered nature. When yet another rap landed on the door, her backbone stiffened and she flung it wide. It was Giannis, and his appearance right there on her doorstep startled her—because she had assumed that Nemos had arrived merely to chauffeur her to some restaurant. Evidently the Greek tycoon had been waiting in his limousine.

Giannis ran his devouring gaze over her lovely face, his attention lingering on her vivid green eyes and the pillowy fullness of her pink mouth. Her lily-white skin and the long curling streamers of crackling Titian hair falling round her shoulders drew him like a magnet. Every time he had relaxed his mental discipline in the past couple of days she had featured in an erotic daydream, and he was not disappointed now, with the reality of her lush, extravagant femininity. Even without couture trappings she was a total babe.

He took immediate advantage of her distracted backward step to press the door wider with a fluid skim of his fingers and stroll in. But he was taken aback by his first view of the poorly furnished, dingy bedsit in which she lived. It had been a long time since he had had contact with such poverty. The chasm between their respective social positions had never been more obvious. But Giannis was where he wanted to be, and it would take the equivalent of an avalanche to send him off course.

Maddie was transfixed by his arrival. He towered over her like a golden Greek god. The pace of her heartbeat rose to a pounding thud in her eardrums. From the ebony darkness of his hair to the gilded bronze of his eyes, set above the smooth, high jut of his stunning cheekbones, he utterly dazzled her. His slate-grey designer suit was the epitome of perfect grooming. He looked devastatingly handsome. He also made her remember the disturbed nights she had endured and the wicked forbidden dreams that constantly replayed the passion she was desperate to forget. Her mortification at the tenor of her thoughts was intense.

'Nemos declined to explain your non-appearance,' he proffered lazily.

The rich, dark timbre of his accented drawl snapped Maddie out of her nervous paralysis. Affronted by the acknowledgement that she had been gaping at him like a country hick, she lifted her chin at a challenging angle. 'What explanation do you need? I don't want to have lunch with you—'

From the first, Giannis had appreciated her beauty, but her plain speech and lack of affectation had added to her attractions. Now, sensual impatience lanced through him. He found her behaviour incomprehensible when all he wanted to do was get her back into his bed again. He was eager to sate the savage ache of desire that had built up while he was abroad on business.

'I told you that I didn't want you to call me,' Maddie completed doggedly, her hands curling into tense fists by her sides.

'You also kissed me,' he countered, brilliant dark eyes lowering with slow, measured provocation to her luscious pink mouth.

Her pale, perfect skin flamed and her silky brown lashes

dropped to screen her guilty eyes. 'That…er…that, like everything else that happened between us, was a mistake—'

'Nonsense, *glikia mou,*' Giannis proclaimed in unapologetic disagreement, his tone of command and conviction as instinctive as his inability to accept defeat.

His cast-iron confidence incensed Maddie. 'It was a mistake for *me*!'

Giannis elevated an ebony brow. 'You have a boyfriend?'

Maddie was insulted that he could think her capable of such a betrayal. 'No! If I had had, I wouldn't have behaved as I did with you.'

'Of course you would have. All women cheat…when a better prospect comes along,' Giannis incised with immovable cynicism.

Her angry distaste made her stand even straighter. 'Maybe the kind of women you're used to mixing with. *I* am not like that.'

His lean, darkly handsome features turned taut and hard. 'Perhaps not. After all, you do harbour the distinction of having had me as your first lover.'

That he had registered that she had been a virgin came as a shock to Maddie, and an embarrassing one at that. To have that truth flung in her face hurt, and his insolent attitude could only heighten her regret over their short-lived intimacy.

'I don't regard it as a distinction.' The flame of anger she had been controlling in a forlorn effort to be dignified had been fanned into a blaze. 'Nor is it a fact I'm likely to want to talk about. No woman would want to boast about having slept with a guy as insensitive as you are!'

Giannis had come into contact with that word 'insensitive' before, but it had only been hinted at, or whispered playfully, and at the first suggestion of a frown had been swiftly smoothed over with plenty of sex. Never before had it been flung at his even white teeth. A warning glint of simmering gold entered his usually level black gaze.

'You're annoyed that I didn't phone you,' he murmured with silken derision. 'I'm a busy guy, and I make no apology for the fact.'

His very intonation was like a red rag to a bull for Maddie. Every syllable he spoke seemed to touch a raw nerve inside her and she bristled, green eyes brightening to emerald chips above her flushed cheekbones. 'I suspect that you don't apologise for very much in life. Obviously people let you get away with being rude and offensive and arrogant—'

'Don't forget insensitive,' Giannis Petrakos purred in helpful addition, while his scorching golden eyes rested on her with raw incredulity. No woman had ever dared to criticise or insult him in such a way. Outraged though he was, he still could not quite believe that she was addressing him with such disrespect.

'Yes—and that too!' Maddie gasped, letting anger become the vent for her emotional turmoil. 'Out of the blue you send an employee to tell me I'm going to have lunch with you…you don't even bother asking…and then you send him back to pick me up. You act and you talk like you're doing me a big favour. Are you so used to women falling over themselves to please you that you just assume I'm the same?'

It was exactly what Giannis was accustomed to. But torture would not have persuaded him to own up to the fact. In a graceful movement he shifted closer, invading her personal space with alacrity. He was seething with anger. He curled a purposeful hand to her chin and tipped up her face. His smouldering gaze clashed head-on with her startled upward glance.

'You gave me good cause, *glikia mou*,' he told her, his Greek accent roughening the delivery of every word.

Her nostrils flared at the faint exotic aroma of the designer cologne he used. Locked to his fierce appraisal, she was shocked to feel a pronounced prickle of sexual awareness travelling through her like a contained electric shock. Her nipples pouted and pushed against the lacy cups of her bra and she tensed in dismay. 'I—'

'And the invitation is still there in every look you give me—because the sex was fantastic,' Giannis intoned thickly.

Her memory flung up an explicit image of his lean, powerful body engulfing hers, and the pain of initiation which had been followed by the waves of hot, piercing pleasure. But even as she helplessly responded, as though he had programmed her, she was shocked by his earthy candour. *The sex was fantastic.* Not exactly a solid base on which to build romantic girlie dreams, she thought painfully.

'And that's all you want.'

Giannis anchored a hand briefly in the luxuriant fall of her rippling curls and intoned steadily, 'I want you. Whatever that entails.'

With a valiant effort Maddie detached herself and pulled back from him, snatching in a gulp of oxygen. She was trembling. 'For how long?'

Giannis shifted graceful lean brown hands in a speaking gesture that asked how he could possibly answer such a question. Watching him, Maddie felt almost mesmerised by his cool sophistication. He was gorgeous, a powerful and masculine work of art. He was out of her league, though— way out. She had already had a taste of how he would treat her. If this was what he was like when he was keen, what would he be like when her attraction had faded? Pride and her usual common sense began to reassert its sway.

'It wouldn't work…it didn't start out right,' she muttered tightly

Sardonic amusement lightened his lean bronzed features. 'Is that the problem? You imagine I might think less of you for matching my passion?'

Maddie shot him an unconvinced glance. 'You don't? You mean, you treat *all* women this way?'

Stung on the raw, Giannis dealt her a fulminating appraisal

But it was wasted on Maddie, who had just realised what time it was and groaned in dismay. 'Oh, my goodness. I'm going to be late for work!'

'Work?' Giannis repeated. 'You work at the weekend as well?'

'Yes.' Snatching up her bag and her overall, Maddie hauled open the door. 'I have to go,' she told him feverishly.

Giannis strode out on to the landing and watched her lock up. 'Where do you work?'

'In the supermarket down the road.' Maddie hurried down the stairs at a rattling pace.

'When do you finish?'

Out on the street, Maddie focused wide-eyed on the opulent black limousine with its tinted windows, and on the number of well-dressed men wearing sunglasses hovering watchfully in its vicinity. The instant Giannis appeared behind her all the men went on visible alert. He was protected everywhere he went. He did not live anything like a normal life. They might as well have been creatures from a different planet, she acknowledged painfully.

'Madeleine?' Giannis prompted drily.

'Six—but what's that got to do with anything?' A rueful laugh fell from her lips. 'Guys like you don't date shopgirls!'

An hour after she started work the flowers arrived. A glorious bouquet of old-fashioned buttery yellow and cream roses was brought to her. Nobody had ever sent her flowers before, and at first she thought there had been a mistake. The sight of her own name on the gift envelope convinced her, however, and she opened the card.

Personally selected and delivered. See you at six, Giannis.

She laughed at that first assurance, and then her face fell. Even had she been tempted she wasn't free this evening. But he didn't quit, and she had always admired that in a man. She thought of what he had done for her dying sister and reminded herself that Giannis Petrakos was very far from being all bad. And she was as much to blame as him for their sexual encounter. Was he right? Was she just angry with him because he hadn't got in touch sooner? She was being torn in two by conflicting promptings, and she felt horribly confused and out of her depth. His arrogance still infuriated her, and she could not shake free of her guilt at having slept with him. Furthermore he was not trying to conceal the fact that only sexual desire drove his continued interest. That was no basis for a relationship—at least not the kind she wanted and needed. So why was she still tempted by him? Why did the gesture of the roses delight her so much?

Half an hour after she got home, Giannis called back for her. 'I never even asked you how you got my address,' she muttered awkwardly, drinking in the sight of his lean bronzed features with strained green eyes.

'Such information is always available for a favour or a price.'

To Maddie, that was yet another unsavoury glimpse of a world and a way of thought foreign to her principles. 'Look, even if I wanted to, I couldn't see you tonight,' she told him hurriedly, keen to bring the conversation to a swift conclusion.

'How so?' he incised, level dark golden eyes pinned to her with questioning force.

There was no apology in Maddie's quiet voice as she explained that she had agreed to sit with her elderly neighbour so that the lady's daughter, who looked after her mother full-time, could enjoy a rare evening out.

'How praiseworthy, *glikia mou*.' A wry smile of approval curved his wide stubborn mouth. 'Naturally I'll organise a qualified carer to stand in for you.'

'No, you can't do that. I never said I would see you tonight, and even if I did want to—which I don't—I wouldn't consider letting my friends down at the last minute,' Maddie declared, her chin coming up at a pugnacious angle because she was indignant at his assumption that she would rearrange her life and her responsibilities to suit him.

But she was even more appalled by her spasm of disappointment that it was not possible for her to consider his offer of providing another companion for her neighbour. She no longer knew what she wanted any more.

Giannis released his breath in a slow, sardonic exhalation. 'Why do you make such a fuss about trivia?'

Maddie was very tense. 'When I make a promise to someone it's not trivial. Mrs Evans would be upset if she was left with a stranger. You are being selfish.'

'Do not insult me again. I will not tolerate it!' the tall, powerful Greek interposed, with cold, cutting emphasis.

Maddie paled and focused on the beautiful roses she had arranged in a utilitarian plastic bowl. Her emotions were all over the place and her eyes were suddenly stinging like mad. 'We're oil and water—'

'Between the sheets we're dynamite.'

A red-hot blush crept up her slender throat and she could not trust herself to look at him. 'You'll have to leave. I have to go down to Mrs Evans.'

'Is this a joke? Or are you wondering how far you can push me?' Giannis demanded with *hauteur*. 'I leave London again tomorrow.'

Reluctantly she lifted her head again, and collided with hot, dark golden eyes that made her tummy lurch as if she had gone down in a lift too fast. 'It's not a joke.'

With languorous cool he let his fingers feather through her long, rippling coppery curls. The faint brush of his fingertips against her taut temples sent a quiver through her, and a feeling of sensual paralysis swallowed up all her good intentions. He brought his darkly handsome head down, and her hand seemed to rise of its own volition to glance across one smooth olive cheek and move into the luxuriant thickness of his black hair. It was all the encouragement he needed. He took her mouth in a storm of passionate hunger and pinned her back against the wall with his lithe, powerful body.

'So what's this?' he enquired lethally.

'Madness,' she mumbled, stretching up on tiptoe to find the heat and hardness of his mouth again in a fruitless attempt to assuage the painful ache low in her belly.

He sank his hands below her curvaceous behind and lifted her, cradling her easily on his lap as he seated himself on the bed. 'How long have you got?' he intoned thickly.

She felt surrounded and controlled by him, and it was incredibly sexy. Her bra was tight over her full breasts, the tender nipples swollen and sensitive. While her body felt weak, her heart was racing with anticipation. She pressed her hot brow against a broad shoulder and wondered frantically what was happening to her. She fought to rescue her self-control. Giannis would take her back to bed if she allowed him to. Was she really *that* besotted with him?

Maddie was shaken by that inner question, and in a sudden movement of denial scrambled off his long, lean thighs with more haste than grace. 'We mustn't… No, absolutely not. Not unless we get to know each other better…' Her voice petered out as a wave of giddiness momentarily left her head swimming.

Giannis sprang upright in an equally abrupt movement, and swung away to stand by the window. He was fully aroused, hotter than hot. Rampant sexual frustration laced the raw sense of disbelief that held him taut. He was not accustomed to suffering that particular discomfort. He could not remember when a woman had last said no to him. The intensity of his desire for her infuriated him. And now she was laying down pre-conditions. Unexpectedly, the fresh taste of that challenge stimulated him. She had backbone and standards. He liked that.

Maddie braced her hand on the table to steady herself. Raw panic threatened to eat her alive because she had never felt so dizzy before. Dizziness was not something she suffered from, so what was causing it? Oh, dear heaven—was it possible that she could be pregnant? How likely was it that she would get symptoms so soon? She scolded herself for overreacting, but the fear she had kept below the surface of her mind for the past few days was now out in the open.

Unfortunately it would be another week before she could put that fear to rest.

'I'll be in Morocco mid-week. I have a house in the High Atlas mountains. It's very private. and peaceful,' Giannis advanced levelly. 'Why don't you let me fly you out to join me for a couple of days?'

'Morocco?' Maddie was astonished by the invitation.

'You said you wanted to get to know me, *glikia mou*.' Giannis drawled, honey-soft. 'It would be the perfect opportunity.'

In a decisive movement he set down his personal card on the table. 'The number of my mobile phone—should you want to contact me.'

CHAPTER FOUR

AS THE helicopter rose in the air at Marrakech-Menara airport, Maddie closed her eyes tight. Unfortunately that exercise made her feel dizzier than ever, and she lifted her lashes and stared woodenly ahead while she prayed that the last leg of her journey would be brief. Maybe she had a problem with her balance? Or perhaps she wasn't eating sensibly enough? It would be paranoid for her to assume that she was in the early stages of pregnancy. She reminded herself that in just a couple of days she would be able to stop worrying, because she had very regular menstrual cycle.

Maddie had flown out from London first thing that morning. It was now after midday, and hot. The long-sleeved shirt and cotton trousers she had worn to travel were sticking to her damp skin. The cloudless sky was a glorious deep lilac-blue. In a covert movement she pinched her thigh, in the hope that the tiny pain would help her to believe that she had indeed come to Morocco as the personal guest of a Greek billionaire. So far nothing about the trip had felt real, since it bore no resemblance to her only previous venture abroad—a package tour to Spain with her grandmother.

On this occasion, however, Maddie was travelling in

amazing style and comfort. Collected from her bedsit by Nemos, she had been the sole passenger on a private jet with a crew who had been almost embarrassingly eager to ensure that she enjoyed the flight. Having watched a terrific film, she had browsed through the morning papers and enjoyed an appetising breakfast while being waited on hand and foot. On landing she had been whisked through official channels at wondrous speed and escorted to a helipad.

Now the helicopter landed, and the merciless ear-battering whine of the propellers finally stilled. Nemos helped Maddie out with care. Initially engaged in adjusting to walking a straight line on solid ground again, she was unprepared for her first sight of the imposing building in front of her. Its sheer size made her stop dead. Soaring ochre walls decorated with geometric patterns were further embellished with slender tapering towers at each corner. Her eyes were wide with astonishment.

'It looks like a Moorish palace.'

'It did once belong to the Caid of the Jerid Valley,' the older man replied. 'But it was a ruin when Mr Petrakos bought it.'

'It's amazing. He must come here a lot.'

'The boss owns a lot of property. It's been a while since he was here.'

In the entrance hall, a jade-coloured fountain was playing down into a pool patterned with mosaics. The water was scattered with rose petals. Nemos introduced her to a Berber manservant, Hamid, who appeared to command a very large staff. He addressed her in French. It was a huge building, designed round a central courtyard ornamented with date palms and flowering vines in a lush tangle of greenery. The interior of the house was cool and opulent and impossibly chic. Ancient carved doors, delicate fretwork wooden screens and painted ceilings provided a backdrop for stylish furniture and extravagant comfort. Shown upstairs by two maids, Maddie walked through double doors set in an arch in the shape of a keyhole, and was immediately convinced that she had been transported into the land of an Arabian Nights fantasy.

Across the vast room a sumptuous bed festooned with gold drapes and tassels sat on a dais. 'My word…' Maddie whispered in wonderment.

With a youthful air of showmanship, one of the pretty dark-eyed maids tugged back the Indian silk drapes and cast open the tall French windows. A roof terrace stretched beyond, but it was the utterly breathtaking view of a fertile green valley ringed by snow-capped mountains that captivated Maddie. A silver basin was placed for her to wash her hands, and mint tea was served in a dainty glass cup before a light meal was brought.

Maddie wondered nervously when Giannis would arrive. Catching a glimpse of her creased and travel-weary appearance in the mirror above the beautiful mother-of-pearl inlaid chest of drawers, she winced. In the equally large adjoining bathroom, the maid was already running water into a luxurious sunken bath. While she scattered fragrant crystals on the surface, her companion laid out a mountain of snowy white towels. When everything was ready for her, Maddie thanked the girls in her rusty schoolgirl French and closed the door to undress. First she went into the steam shower, where she took a while to get acquainted with the elaborate technology before she could comfortably wash her hair. Then, her wet hair piled on top of her head, she sank into the bath and tried to relax.

In truth, she was as tense as a drawn knife. She did not quite know what had brought her to Morocco. The fact that Giannis had offered her the chance to get to know him just as she had asked? That it would have been downright contrary to refuse such an offer? Or had her decision been influenced by the fear that she might be pregnant? Was that what was making her feel so connected to him? Or was she just lying to herself and making silly excuses in a forlorn effort to avoid facing the embarrassing truth?

From the moment she had seen Giannis Petrakos in his office she had been virtually obsessed by him. The fact that he had once been the unwitting target of her adolescent crush had made her even more susceptible to his vibrant, dark good looks. She had fallen into bed with him because she could not resist him, and she was in Morocco for the same reason. *There,* she reflected heavily, she was finally being honest with herself. Only being honest made her feel infinitely more vulnerable.

What did she have in common with a guy who owned a palace in Morocco that he rarely visited? Evidently he had as many options in property as he must surely have with women. Where did she fit in? For the first time she was curious about her predecessors. What sort of women did Giannis get involved with? Was she typical? Suddenly she wished she could afford to buy the kind of magazines which featured photos and features on the lifestyles of the very rich. But, curious though she was, she knew that she would not be buying any such publications in the near future. She had taken three days out from working and earning—a decision that would ensure she was living right on the breadline for the next month.

When Maddie emerged from the bathroom in a towel, she was ushered into yet another connecting room, where a smiling English-speaking beautician and her assistant were waiting to offer a bewildering range of treatments. Disconcerted by the situation, Maddie agreed to have a massage because she really didn't know how to keep on saying no without causing offence. Fragrant rose-scented oils were rubbed into her skin in what ultimately proved to be a wonderfully relaxing experience. She then allowed the talented duo to style her hair and do her nails. Afterwards, she felt amazingly sleepy. Although she could not find her case, a gossamer-light turquoise silk kaftan was draped on the bed. Too weary to go looking for her clothes, she put it on and lay down for a nap.

When Krista Spyridou called Giannis that same day, his jet had stopped off to refuel in Paris.

'I've come up with a new theme for the wedding,' his fiancée announced happily.

Giannis grimaced.

'Antony and Cleopatra!' Krista gushed.

'What a killer precedent that would be,' Giannis told her. 'Anthony and Cleopatra's marriage was bigamous.'

'I don't believe you!' she wailed. 'They didn't show that in the movie I saw.'

'Anthony already had a Roman wife.' Impatience gripped Giannis as Krista lamented that news as seriously as if he had just informed her of a death. Had he ever seen her read a book? Discuss anything remotely intelligent? Giannis frowned. She had yawned when he'd taken her to visit an archaeological dig at one of his properties in Athens. The sheer depth of her ignorance was starting to irritate him.

By the time Giannis arrived at his remote fortress hideaway in Morocco the sun was casting arrow-shaped shadows through the intricate window screens. He spoke to Hamid in

Arabic. Ascending the winding staircase, he strolled into the master bedroom suite as smoothly as a leopard on the prowl, and came to a halt only when he saw Maddie lying on top of the vast bed. Her flame-coloured hair was streaming like a banner of silk off the pillows, her pale, delicate profile marked by the prominence of her voluptuous pink mouth. Her low neckline exposed the deep cleavage between the snowy white slopes of her full, round breasts. The rich, ripe curve of her bottom strained against the fine silk fabric. The instant rush of blood to his groin almost hurt. He was enthralled by her sex appeal and the intensity of his desire.

'Maddie…?' he murmured, using the diminutive for the first time.

Shifting position, Maddie opened her eyes and saw him standing several feet away. Her breath snarled up in her throat. He needed a shave. The shadow of dark stubble over his strong jaw, however, only enhanced the hard masculinity of his lean bronzed features. She raised herself on one elbow. 'I must've fallen asleep.'

Giannis took off his gold silk-lined jacket and tossed it on a chair with easy grace. 'I was held up in Paris…my apologies. But it's wonderful to find you here waiting for me, *glikia mou*.'

For a split second Maddie didn't quite follow his meaning, and then his confident path round the very grand and elegant room pitched her brain back into gear. 'This is *your* room…er…*your* bed?'

A wolfish smile slashed his wide stubborn mouth. 'You sound like Goldilocks.'

Her colour heightened because she felt very foolish. 'I didn't realise. I should've guessed.'

The gilded bronze brilliance of his gaze glinted below his

dense black lashes. 'Don't tell me I've flown halfway round the world to be exiled to a guest suite?'

Picking up on that measured tone of male disbelief, Maddie scrambled up on her knees, anxious to take the heat out of the situation. 'No, I'll use a guestroom—'

'Over my dead body,' Giannis incised without hesitation, when she dared to float that proposition. 'You stay. We share. At the very least I will hold you in my arms through the night.'

'But I thought—'

His stubborn jawline clenched. 'And I thought otherwise,' he cut in with ruthless purpose. 'So we must compromise. I'm a very physical guy, and it is possible that you are asking me to be something I can't.'

Although her face was hot, Maddie breathed in very deep and looked levelly back at him. 'You have such a forceful personality,' she told him gently. 'But I'm sure you don't mean to put pressure on me.'

The silence simmered like a cauldron on the boil. An almost imperceptible rise of dark blood warmed the imperious slant of Giannis Petrakos's classic cheekbones. 'Naturally not.'

'Of course, if you feel I've come out here on false pretences, 'Maddie added uncomfortably, 'I'll understand if you think I should leave.'

It was a very rare experience for Giannis, but that unexpected suggestion totally silenced him. She was not voicing her offer as a threat that he could condemn as sexual blackmail. She appeared genuinely awkward and unhappy, and that contrived to touch both his strong pride and his sense of honour. He was too macho a man to like the suggestion that he might use his potent strength of character to ride roughshod over her reservations about sleeping with him again.

Irritated though he was, he was still not prepared to let her go and replace her with a more sycophantic female. Madeleine Conway had haunted his thoughts for the best part of an incredibly frustrating week, and the past few days had only been rendered bearable by the knowledge that she would be waiting for him in Morocco.

'*Ohi*…no, that will not be necessary,' Giannis conceded in a driven undertone, his lapse into his native Greek an indicator of his more volatile mood.

'I don't want to leave…this is the most fabulous place,' Maddie confided, glancing up at him from beneath her silky lashes.

The shy provocation of that single glance sent hunger pounding through his lithe, powerful frame. He sank down on the edge of the bed and crushed her lush pink lips under his, his tongue ravishing the tender reaches of her mouth with a carnal skill that made her shake in the strong circle of his arms. 'Why are you making me wait?' he ground out thickly. 'I ache for you.'

Her shapely body was rigid with tension. Her nipples were stiff straining buds that she was afraid were visible beneath the thin silk bodice of the kaftan. She decided that she really did need to get into a less provocative outfit. In an abrupt move that took him by surprise, she slid off the bed. 'I should get dressed now.'

Quick to surmise that she intended to cover as much of her wondrous hourglass shape as possible, away from his appreciative gaze, Giannis entrapped her hand in his larger one to prevent her from moving away. Instinct warned him that she was skittish, and it was not the moment to tell her that the dressing room would be packed tight with the generous array of designer apparel he had ordered for her enjoyment. 'No. Don't change. You look relaxed, and that's one of the things I like about you. You don't fuss about your hair, or your face, or your clothes. We'll have dinner on the terrace.'

Maddie had neither expected nor received anything much in the way of praise in her life. What she hadn't known she hadn't missed. When she was a child, circumstances had made her more of a bystander than a main player, and even after she had grown up other people's needs had continued to take precedence. That single compliment from Giannis had a quite disproportionate effect on her, and gave her a warm squishy feeling inside. *One of the things I like about you.* At that moment, even if she had been wearing a bin-bag, she would have stayed dressed in it for his benefit. And, had she had sufficient nerve, she would have made him list every single other tiny thing he liked about her.

Giannis swept up the house phone and spoke in a foreign language. Tossing it aside again, he began peeling off his shirt. 'I need a shower.'

Her attention locked on his bare bronzed shoulders and his powerful hair-roughened chest. When he stretched muscles rippled below his tawny skin, and her gaze was drawn down to the hard taut slab of his flat stomach. She had never looked at a man like that before, had never even been tempted, but she found it exceedingly difficult to drag her regard from him. Her palms tingled in recollection of the satin smooth feel of his damp back beneath her fingers.

Giannis caught her looking at him and recognised her rapt appreciation for what it was. '*Theos*…little fraud, you are as hungry for me as I am for you!'

Wildly embarrassed, Maddie flushed to the roots of her

hair and parted her lips to protest the point. How had he guessed? How could he possibly have known what she was thinking about?

'Deny it at your peril,' Giannis warned in a husky tone of intimacy that sent tiny quivers coursing down her sensitive spine. 'And don't forget that you can't get closer to me by denying us both the natural expression of our desire.'

Having made that lethal point, he left her alone. The instant he vanished she wanted him back within view again. Her natural caution tried to kick in, but it fought a losing battle against the truth that she was simply happy. Happy to be in Morocco, downright ecstatic to be with Giannis. For a moment the strength of those new feelings scared her, and then she gave herself a firm little mental shake. So what if she was no longer the very sensible and calm young woman she had always believed herself to be? If she got hurt, she got hurt. Better to have loved and lost than never to have loved at all, she told herself with determined cheer.

Her feet shod in the light embroidered slippers she'd discovered by the bed, Maddie went out to the sun-baked terrace. The heat of the day was now ebbing. A great stained glass dome of rich jewelled colours formalised a shaded seating area that was furnished with sumptuous sofas and a marble table already set with fine porcelain and crystal. Offered a drink by Hamid, she opted for fruit juice and curled up on an opulent cushioned couch to catch up with a newspaper article she had begun reading on her flight.

'What are you reading about?'

Black hair still spiky from the shower, Giannis was strolling towards her in tailored cream chinos and an open-necked striped shirt.

Maddie named a British politician who had been caught cheating on his long-suffering wife for the second time in as many months. 'I hope his wife chucks him out.' Shaking her bright head, she sighed, 'Infidelity is so sleazy.'

Lean, darkly handsome face uninformative, Giannis came to a slow halt. 'Not always.'

'You can't mean that.' Maddie was taken aback by his response, for it was a subject she felt strongly about. 'Look at all the lies and deception that go hand in hand with infidelity. It causes so much misery. Just imagine what that man's poor wife and teenage children must be going through right now—'

'It is regrettable,' Giannis pronounced flatly.

'It's *more* than regrettable,' Maddie stressed, jumping to her feet. 'It's wrong! My mother cheated on my father with his best friend. It totally destroyed Dad. I would never betray anyone's trust. Honesty is always the best policy, and loyalty means a great deal to me.'

Lush black lashes screened his brilliant dark eyes to a cool glimmer. 'I can see that.'

'If you weren't single, believe me, I wouldn't be here,' Maddie added, keen to draw a stronger response from him.

Hamid was hovering with the first course. Mastering his stark disconcertion at what he had just discovered, Giannis waved the manservant forward and urged Maddie to sit down again. A procession of dishes was brought to the table while Giannis reappraised the situation. Maddie didn't know he was engaged.

He had simply assumed that the whole world knew he was engaged to Krista Spyridou. His fiancée had certainly gone to extraordinary lengths to publicise their engagement. A Greek television channel had even made a reality documentary about the couple, full of truly cringe-worthy stuff that had been shown round half the world. But Maddie had no idea whatsoever.

Of course he would have to tell her, Giannis acknowledged grimly. Right at that very moment, however, it struck him as a likely case of suicidally bad timing. Just after she got down from her fidelity soapbox was not the perfect opportunity to announce that he was engaged to be married to another woman. Particularly when Maddie had already slept with him. Particularly when he was fully committed to the goal of persuading her that she could have a terrific future as his mistress.

'Your take on morals is young and idealistic,' Giannis remarked lazily. 'My great-grandmother would be in firm agreement with you, but then she's over ninety years old and her values are etched in solid stone.'

Maddie tilted her chin. 'I suppose I am a little old-fashioned, but time and experience won't alter my views,' she replied. 'What's the rest of your family like?'

His lean, strong face shuttered. 'I have an enormous tribe of relations.'

'You are *so* lucky.' Maddie tucked into her food with an appetite and enthusiasm that brought a reluctant smile to his sardonic mouth. He was accustomed to women who barely ate in his presence. 'I've got nobody close left, and I really miss having a family.'

Giannis watched her thank the serving staff. She was a very beautiful but essentially ordinary girl, with an extraordinary amount of personal warmth and charm. Was it her very ordinariness that attracted him? Was that the novelty that, against all the odds, kept him coming back for more? In bed she was red-hot. That was what made her so essential to his comfort, he decided with a sense of relief. It was just sex—and why not? She might not fit into his world, but he wanted her there, and what he wanted he would have. Whatever it took, whatever it cost.

Coloured glass lanterns glowed as the sun went down in a sky shot with a wonderful rainbow of colours. He entertained her with the story of how he had stumbled on the ruined Casbah when he was a teenager on a mountain-climbing expedition with friends. 'My every wrong move was making global headlines that year. I thought this would make a great secret location for wild weekend parties.'

Maddie blinked. 'Are you serious?'

'Partying was a serious part of my upbringing. My parents never did anything that didn't amuse them.' Giannis was amused by her consternation. 'On my second visit with the architect, the local headman invited me to visit his village across the valley. The people were very poor. They needed the employment I could provide, but the wild parties would have made it impossible for most of them to work for me.'

'So you decided not to have the parties?'

'I got into extreme sports instead,' he murmured, with a casual shrug of dismissal. 'Much healthier.'

But Maddie gave him a huge smile, because she was finally catching a glimpse of the guy who had made it his mission to ensure that her dying sister's teenage dream came true. She knew that some day she would tell him about that, and identify herself, but right then she didn't want to open a sad subject. Nor did she want to figure in his mind as the grateful and admiring adolescent whom he hadn't even noticed at the time.

A light breeze feathered through the silk kaftan she wore

and she shivered, surprised by how much the temperature seemed to have dropped. 'It's getting chilly out here.'

'Desert nights are cold in the spring.' Giannis closed his hand over hers to urge her back indoors.

One step inside the softly lit bedroom, she decided that she wanted to share the bed with him in every sense of the word. It was too late to be taking fright and trying to turn the clock back, she reasoned frantically, engaged in a last-ditch battle with her misgivings. What was the point of raising such an artificial barrier between them? Was it even honest or fair, when she too longed to experience that intimacy again?

Her bright copper head downbent, she stilled and plucked abstractedly at one of the handmade buttons on his shirt. Sudden shyness almost overpowered her; it was a challenge to ask him to make love to her when he had been so circumspect throughout the evening.

'I don't need to wait any more,' she said finally, wincing at herself even as she spoke.

On a high at that unexpected declaration, Giannis startled her by reaching down and sweeping her right off her feet and up into his strong arms. 'I will spend the next twenty-four hours in bed with you, *pedhi mou*!'

'Go easy,' she urged in embarrassment. 'Be careful—'

'*Careful?*' Brilliant golden eyes collided with hers, his luxuriant black lashes lifting in a request for her to expand on her meaning.

'The accident with the contraception,' she reminded him uneasily.

'A once-in-a-lifetime event. Surely you're not still worrying about that?' Giannis censured, with the supreme confidence of a male who took it for granted that life always went his way. 'Are you late?'

'No...but—'

'You'll be okay. Don't look for trouble.' He lowered her down onto the bed with a slow-burning smile that convinced her that her worries were quite unnecessary.

CHAPTER FIVE

GIANNIS threaded his lean brown fingers through Maddie's tumbling auburn tresses to tug her head back. His hot golden gaze connected with hers on a shaft of pure sensual force.

'I promise that you won't regret choosing to be with me,' he breathed thickly. 'I will give you a life such as you have never dreamt of.'

'But I don't need you to give me anything.' Even as Maddie declared that she was wondering what he meant, but just then she found that she could not concentrate. Other much more physical responses were taking over.

Giannis began to flip loose the tiny pearl buttons on the bodice of her kaftan. Her breath shortened in her throat. Her breasts ached, the soft pink peaks tensing into protruding points. Between her thighs she felt a tiny pulse flicker and throb into being, and she stiffened, instinctively ashamed of the depth of her wanton craving.

'I hope you have no objection to the gift of pleasure?' Giannis teased, fiercely aroused and rejoicing in her explosive effect on his libido.

'Pleasure's f-fine,' she stammered, as he folded back the

parted edges of the kaftan fabric and exposed the burgeoning swell of her creamy rose-tipped breasts.

'As tender as velvet.' His voice was hoarse as he chafed her sensitive nipples between finger and thumb. With a groan of satisfaction, he cupped her lush, full breasts and lowered his dark head to suckle the swollen crests. Pleasure engulfed her in a drenching wave, extracting whimpers of formless sound from her parted lips.

In a fluid movement he leant back from her and pulled off his shirt, springing upright to remove his trousers. Her heart racing, a languorous weakness gripping her limbs, she lay back against the pillows, watching him. His chinos hit the rug. She was madly curious, and she couldn't stop looking. He was as confident in his own naked skin as he was in a business suit. And that sleek self-assurance was as sexy as the appeal of his strong, hard body. He discarded his boxers and strolled back to the bed. The bold length of his virile masculinity made her gulp.

Enjoying the wide-eyed visual appraisal she was trying so hard and unsuccessfully to hide, Giannis dealt her a wolfish grin. 'Do I meet your expectations?'

'Who am I supposed to compare you to?' Maddie riposted, hot-cheeked.

The aggressive strength of will that powered the continual expansion of his massive business empire hardened his lean strong face. 'No other man. You belong with me now.'

'Women don't *belong* to men in this century.'

'Would you feel right doing this with someone else?' Giannis enquired, sliding deft hands below her hips and tugging her kaftan off.

She was caught between dismay at that concept and self-consciousness at her nudity. 'No, of course not. But—'

'You take my point so beautifully, *glikia mou*.' Giannis leant hungrily over her to taste her luscious mouth.

He used his tongue to make a darting foray between her lips, and a snaking spasm of response clenched low in her pelvis. He buried his expert mouth in the hollow beneath her collarbone before lowering his head to let his teeth graze her distended nipples. A low gasp broke from her. Her skin dampened. A delicious yearning was drumming up the honeyed heat at the secret heart of her. Her fingers curved round a smooth brown shoulder, and when he slid up level with her again she explored the solid muscular wall of his chest, traced the silky furrow of hair that led down to his straining sex.

'Show me what you like,' she whispered unevenly.

Giannis told her in the most succinct terms, and took great pleasure in offering guidance. She devoted herself to the new learning experience with an innocent enthusiasm that forced him to conclude the exercise much faster than he had anticipated. Groaning as he fought to reinstate control, he kissed her with devouring hunger. 'You almost pushed me over the edge, *pedhi mou*.'

Making love to him had heightened her desire, and her level of frustration. She quivered in the shelter of his arms, madly aware of the tingling burn of emptiness between her slender thighs. When he sought out the damp heat of that tender triangle, she gritted her teeth to hold back a cry. Her longing was so intense she pressed her face into his shoulder, drinking in the achingly familiar scent of his skin. He shifted, parting her legs to stroke the delicate pink softness of her lush femininity. He rubbed the little pearl of sensation and she moaned and shivered. As the tormenting heat rose, her hips shifted back and forth on the mattress. Paying no heed to her protests, he employed his mouth with skilful eroticism on her squirming body.

'Giannis…please…'

'If you can still talk, you're not enjoying yourself enough.'

That intimacy was a sweet torment which drove her out of her mind with delight. Wild waves of desperate hunger controlled her. The pressure in her pelvis built and built. She was so hot she was melting, and at the instant where irresistible sensation became sensual torture a shattering climax convulsed her and she abandoned herself to the ecstasy.

Giannis wasted no time in rearranging her limp body and forging a bold passage into her sensitised flesh. He took her with ruthless precision, and she cried out in feverish response. He deepened his penetration, tipping her back at an angle demanding that she take all of him. Frantic excitement enveloped her. His every powerful movement sent ripples of delirious pleasure coursing through her responsive body. He pounded into her with sure, fast strokes. What she had not known could happen again took her a second time, and the frenzied rise of her passionate response swept her to another electrifying orgasm.

'You enthral me, *pedhi mou*.' Giannis rolled back from her and gently straightened her out. He carried her nerveless fingers to his mouth and kissed them. 'That was wonderful.'

Every muscle ached. Her body almost hurt in the aftermath of that huge, demanding flood of pleasure. The air-conditioning was chilling the perspiration from her body and she shivered.

'Cold?' Giannis questioned

'Silly, isn't it?' Maddie muttered.

Giannis didn't like this constraint. It wasn't what he had

anticipated from her. He had thought that she might well fall in love with him. He had half expected her to cling to him with naïve affection, and he had braced himself to tolerate being hugged. But not only had she made no such move, she was also disturbingly quiet. Perhaps she felt unappreciated? he reasoned. As it was his experience that his lovers always expected gifts, he thought that it was now time to show her the designer wardrobe he had ordered for her.

'I'll get you something to put on.' Giannis sprang off the bed.

'I didn't bring a wrap.' Maddie wished she dared suggest that greater proximity would soon warm her up again—he put out sufficient body heat to power an apartment block. In truth, a terrible uncertainty was threatening to claim her again. Now that their one-night stand had turned into an affair, she realised that she didn't know how to go about conducting one. She wanted reassurance that what they had wasn't a casual thing, on his terms, but she knew she was being too needy, looking for too much too soon. There was no way she could risk such questions.

Giannis strolled into the dressing room and rolled back the doors. 'Come here…I want to show you something.'

Maddie lifted his discarded shirt and held it against her in an effort to cover the expanse of her own bare skin. Wondering what the heck he could want to show her, she came to an awkward halt in the doorway.

'All the clothes in here are yours.'

Her delicate brows pleated in confusion. 'How can they be mine?'

Giannis shrugged. 'This is my gift to you. Staff will be standing by tomorrow, to alter anything that doesn't fit.'

Stunned by what he was telling her, Maddie tugged open a drawer and skated a doubtful fingertip over silk and lace lingerie. How dared he buy her underwear? Her small white teeth gritted. She stared at the garments hanging in the closet, noting a very famous designer label and sliding the items along the rail to examine another couple, before drawing back her hands as though she had been stung by a wasp. Mortified colour had washed into her cheeks.

'I can't believe that you think it's okay to do something like this,' she told him tightly, threading her arms into the sleeves of his shirt, because she now felt foolish naked. 'I may not own any fancy clothes, but that doesn't mean I want you to buy them for me!'

'My only motivation was to please you.'

'Did you pick them out personally?' she asked abruptly.

In the act of pulling out a pair of jeans from the other side of the dressing room, Giannis tensed, recalling another débâcle when he had sent Nemos to her door to organise lunch. 'No.'

'Did you describe what you wanted?'

'I may have mentioned a favourite colour or two.'

'Mine or yours?'

'I don't know yours,' he was forced to admit, his handsome mouth taut with impatience. He zipped the jeans. What was her problem? Why couldn't she be grateful, as so many other women had been before her? Why was she so outrageously difficult to please?

'Which really says it all, doesn't it?' Maddie snapped. 'You don't know my favourite colours and you don't really care either. You want to dress me up like a fashion doll for *your* benefit, not mine.'

His dark golden eyes simmered. 'That is untrue.'

'If you don't like me as I am, tough!' Maddie flung at him,

her generous mouth curling with pained defiance. 'And at least have the sensitivity to appreciate that spending thousands and thousands of pounds on someone like me, just because you've slept with them, gives a very insulting message!'

That concluding crack made Giannis furious. Slashing his hands through the air in a striking gesture of exasperation, he strode back into the bedroom. 'So we're back to the missing sensitivity gene?'

'I do not need to be reminded that you're richer than sin.'

'Stop talking as though my wealth is a serious flaw,' Giannis sliced back with sardonic bite.

'But it *is*…can't you see that? It's a barrier between us. I'm not a hooker you need to pay—but that's how you're making me feel! '

'*Theos mou*…You're such a diva!' Giannis condemned, colder than ice. 'A gift is not an insult, and it should be accepted with grace. I'm a generous man and your attitude is offensive. You have no idea of how to behave. And, by the way, no hooker would make as little effort to please as you do!'

His censure cut deep. Tears prickled and stung the backs of her eyes, for she was not in the habit of staging violent arguments—nor had she ever been told before that she lacked manners. She shrank inside his shirt. But she still felt it would be wrong to accept that vast collection of shockingly expensive clothes. She wasn't a hired entertainer. Wearing garments purchased by him would only serve to increase her sense of inequality. But maybe if she wore his gifts to mask that big financial difference he would feel more comfortable with her? a little inner voice suggested. So who was right…and who was wrong?

Her head buzzing with conflicting thoughts, she walked out

on to the roof terrace. Chilled by the night air, she curled up in a heap on a couch. A few minutes later a maid came out, to offer her an opulent cashmere rug.

Giannis watched from the bedroom while Maddie wrapped herself up in the rug he'd had sent out to her. His strong jawline clenched. Nobody else argued with him—and never, ever a woman. What made her so feisty? So critical of him? She was annoying the hell out of him.

In one of the lightning-fast decisions that made him so formidable an opponent in the business world, Giannis rammed the French windows back from his path and went outside. In the light from the coloured glass lanterns her green eyes shone with the clarity of jewels. Without hesitation—for he was determined to overcome any objections—Giannis bent down, scooped her up, complete with rug, and went back indoors with her again.

'What on earth are you doing?' Maddie squealed in disconcertion.

Settling her back on the bed, Giannis followed her down in one lithe movement. Bare-chested, long powerful legs clad only in well-worn faded jeans, he stared down at her in mocking challenge. 'What do you think?'

'You said I'd no manners—'

Long brown fingers shaped her high cheekbones. Fierce dark golden eyes assailed hers. 'I thought you'd be thrilled with a new wardrobe.'

Her soft mouth down-curved; her long brown lashes dipped. 'I'm sorry…I didn't think of it from your point of view.'

'Or I from yours. You're different from other women. But that's why I want you so much. ' Giannis let his wide sensual mouth drift down on hers like a caress.

As the kiss deepened the hot, hungry taste of his urgency intoxicated her. The feverish thoughts tugging her in different directions subsided. Liquid warmth uncoiled in her belly. His long, powerful body came down on hers, acquainting her with the deliciously aggressive thrust of his erection. A helpless frisson of response rippled through her and centred on the ache stirring in her pelvis. Suddenly she wanted him again, with the most shocking ferocity…

The following day, Maddie stirred drowsily and sent a seeking hand across the bed for Giannis. Finding only empty space, she opened her eyes. The bathroom door wasn't quite closed, and she could hear the thump of water on tiles: he was in the shower. She peered at her watch with a softened smile. It was four in the afternoon.

Earlier that day Giannis had flown her to Marrakech, for breakfast in a fabulous old hotel, before taking her for a visit to the souks. Momentarily her face clouded. She'd had to struggle to hide the fact that the strong, aromatic scents of the spice market had made her feel nauseous. She suppressed the lingering stab of concern, since she could not help but be influenced by Giannis's sublime conviction that their contraceptive mishap would have no consequences. They had returned to his mountain hideaway for lunch on the almond terrace, where they had sat beneath trees weighed down with exquisite clouds of spring blossom. Long before the final course arrived they had left the table to make love again.

His mobile phone buzzed on the bedside cabinet. She had noticed that he never missed a call. After a moment's hesitation she reached out and answered it. A flood of words in another language made her appreciate the pointlessness of her attempt to be helpful.

'I'm sorry…can I help you?' she asked in apologetic English.

'Who are you? Some little secretary bird?' the female demanded haughtily. 'Put me on to my fiancé.'

Maddie frowned in confusion. 'Your fiancé? Who do I say is calling?'

'Krista. Who else?' the woman responded with withering scorn. 'Hurry up…I haven't got all day!'

Maddie set the phone down with a weak hand. She discovered that she couldn't seem to catch her breath. She was as winded as though she had been punched in the gut. It had to be some misunderstanding. Or perhaps the woman had been joking, or lying for some reason best known to her? What the heck was she imagining? That Giannis would deceive her to that extent? That she could be so foolish? She realised with a sinking heart that she had never actually asked him if there was anyone else in his life. But he *knew* that she believed he was single, she reminded herself frantically, thinking back to their conversation the night before.

Sliding out of bed, she reached for the turquoise kaftan she had been using as a dressing gown. As she pulled it on with clumsy hands she heard an angry burst of speech from the phone she had laid down.

Giannis appeared with a towel twisted round his lean brown hips. She pointed at the receiver. 'Krista's on the phone.'

He was still only for a fraction of a second, and his lean, darkly handsome features betrayed nothing. Yet Maddie knew in that same instant that there was no misunderstanding, no joke, and no lie: the guy she had allowed herself to fall madly in love with was engaged to another woman. Her skin felt cold and clammy. Shock was setting like pointed shards of ice in her stomach. He was speaking Greek on the phone, but somehow his dark-timbred drawl sounded to her as though it was coming from the other end of a long dark tunnel. Through him she had learned to recognise the sound of his language. Did Krista speak Greek as well? Hastily she tried to shut out that thought. Because she wasn't ready to think about the unfortunate woman whom she had inadvertently wronged.

Giannis raked a keen-eyed glance at Maddie. She was as pale as death, her Titian hair like a burning firebrand against the pallor of her alabaster skin. He could not concentrate on the conversation with Krista, which related, as usual, to her latest selection of extravagantly inappropriate wedding themes. His lean, powerful face set with purpose, he brought the call to a swift close and swung back to Maddie.

'This is not the way you should have found out about Krista,' Giannis conceded. 'But until you came to Morocco I believed that you already knew of her existence. My engagement is common knowledge.'

'But you should have told me.' Her voice almost failed her, because with every word he spoke the nightmare became more real, and more agonising for her to bear.

'I intended to tell you when you got back to London.'

Maddie parted near bloodless lips. 'After you'd had your fun?' she slotted in tightly, a deep sense of humiliation creeping over her. 'How long have you been engaged?'

'A couple of months. I see no reason why it should come between us.'

Maddie was too shattered by what she had found out to do more than shake her head in incomprehension at that bold statement. The conversation had already knocked her off balance, since he was not reacting as she had assumed he would. He was not apologising, he was not making excuses. Indeed, he was not even owning up to his fault.

'I want you to take the time to consider the fact that what I have with Krista is quite separate from what I have with you.'

A mortified laugh that carried no humour fell jarringly from Maddie's dry lips. 'I hardly need to be told that. I may not be very sophisticated, but even I can tell the difference between an engagement ring and the equivalent of a dirty weekend!'

His big powerful body tensed. 'That is not how it has been between us.'

'How would I know how it's been when I've been in the dark ever since the first day?' Maddie demanded feverishly. 'Why did you involve me in this horrible situation? And why did you bother getting engaged if you don't intend to be faithful?'

'Perhaps fidelity is not as important to some people as it is to you,' Giannis delivered. 'I will only say that my conscience is clear as far as my engagement is concerned.'

'Well, bully for you…so your fiancée was desperate enough to take you on those terms? Presumably she made that choice.' Maddie watched his lean strong face tighten with hauteur and marvelled at his self-assurance, his stubborn refusal to acknowledge that he had done wrong. 'But I didn't get that opportunity. You *lied* to me—'

'I have told no lies,' Giannis asserted.

'You lied to me by omission.' Angry patches of colour had blossomed in Maddie's cheeks. 'Last night you *knew* I didn't know you were engaged when I said I wouldn't be with you if you weren't single. But you chose not to tell me the truth.'

'We had already slept together. I didn't see the point of upsetting you when you were away from home.'

That was the precise point at which Maddie lost her temper, for it seemed to her that he had the hide of a rhinoceros. 'In other words, you put your own comfort first and decided that it was fine to leave me in ignorance. It didn't matter to you that I was betraying *my* values in getting involved with a man who's planning to marry another woman. Or that the knowledge that our relationship is not an exclusive one makes me feel physically sick!'

His lean, dark face hardened, his strong jawline squaring. 'Of course it matters to me. But one cannot live one's whole life by rigid rules—'

'Particularly not when they conflict with what Giannis Petrakos wants?' Maddie dared. 'There are good reasons for the rules I live by.'

Giannis studied her with glittering golden eyes. 'I want you more than I've wanted any woman for a very long time. Walking away wasn't an option.'

'Let's not exaggerate my supposed attraction,' Maddie cut in rawly, a pain as sharp as a knife twisting through her. 'Obviously it's only sex, because my personal appeal won't prevent you from marrying someone else. Yet you talked about *me* not knowing how to behave? Don't you think I had the right to know I was just a casual fling? A little bit on the side of the main event? If you had had any respect for me at all, you wouldn't have treated me like this!'

'You're wrong about that. There was an explosive attraction. Nor do I think that self-denial makes anyone a better person.' With that ringing rejoinder, Giannis went into the dressing room and pulled out fresh clothing. 'We'll discuss this when you've calmed down. I consider arguments a waste of valuable energy.'

'And walking out the ultimate escape hatch,' Maddie told him tightly.

That incendiary comment brought Giannis back into view, his tailored chinos still unbuttoned at his lean waist, his bronzed hair-roughened chest still bare. He refused to consider the rights and wrongs. What was done was done. But he was determined not to lose her. 'I don't do escape hatches.'

'It doesn't matter. Just arrange for me to get home as soon as possible.' She tilted up her chin and drew on every ounce of her pride to hide her pain. 'I don't mind having to sit around the airport for hours and wait for a flight either.'

'This is crazy. Why should you leave? It's nonsense to say that what we have is casual,' Giannis insisted forcefully. 'I want you in my life—'

'Well, I think I can safely say that this is one of those very rare occasions when you don't get what you want.' Green eyes glittering with furious condemnation, Maddie surveyed him.

'I won't let you leave.'

'You have no choice.' Maddie yanked out her overnight bag and devoted her attention to packing the few items she had brought from London. She hated him, but she was terrified that the agony of picturing him in another woman's arms would still kill her by inches. She had to keep busy. Activity and the need to think of practicalities were the only things capable of keeping her sane.

Giannis watched her piling her possessions into an untidy heap. He did not do emotional confrontations, he reminded himself doggedly. He did not do emotions, full-stop. He had never been into love and promises or, for that matter, stories of happily-ever-after. But he knew that she believed in all of those things, and that he had hurt her. He would give her the time and the space to quieten down. He did not believe that she would just walk away from him.

An hour later, Hamid informed him that Maddie was in the salon with her luggage. Giannis stared at the computer screen and realised that he had done no work during that time.

Clad in a simple white shirt and denim skirt, with her glorious hair confined by a band at the nape of her neck, she was standing by the window.

'I realise that you're upset, but there is such a thing as the art of compromise,' Giannis drawled softly.

'Giannis…' Maddie whispered in jagged interruption. 'Compromise would only be another word for you using me, and I'm not a glutton for punishment. But I have decided that everything that's happened isn't entirely your fault. I have to take a share of the blame too.'

His ebony brows pleated. 'Meaning?'

Maddie wanted to tell him about Suzy, because she was convinced that this would be the last time she ever saw him. 'For you to understand, I have to go back nine years in time to when I first saw you. I was fourteen years old.'

Giannis was intrigued. 'The first time? How? Where?'

'You visited my twin sister in a children's hospice.'

Disconcertion made him frown. 'A hospice?'

Her generous mouth compressed. 'Her name was Suzy…and, no, you didn't notice me on either visit. I was just one of the admiring crowd round the tea trolley. My sister had leukaemia and not much time left. A fortnight later you returned and brought her favourite pop pin-up to visit her. She was overjoyed. He was her hero, and that day you became mine for doing it for her.'

Giannis was astonished by what she was telling him. He too had lost a sibling as a teenager, but that was something he never discussed. Furthermore, what she said had cut through even his tough shell and drawn blood. *He was her hero and that day you became mine.* Ten words, and every one the equivalent of a spear in the guts, Giannis conceded grimly. 'Your sister—Suzy—died?'

Her beautiful green eyes sad, Maddie nodded.

'I'm sorry. Over the years I've visited hundreds of children. I'm afraid I don't remember her,' he admitted.

'It's long time ago. I didn't expect you to. I just wanted you to know that, even though everything has gone wrong between us on a personal level, I'll always be grateful for the fact that you made my sister so happy.'

'I don't want you to be grateful, *pedhi mou,*' Giannis breathed in a roughened undertone. 'Gratitude in that field is the one thing I have never sought from anyone.'

'But I hope it explains why I acted so stupidly when I finally got the chance to speak to you. I had this false picture of you—a silly, immature image. I'm sure I gave you the wrong impression.'

His gilded bronze eyes darkened and screened. '*Theos mou*…I don't want to hear this.'

'I must go.' Maddie would not allow herself to look at him again. Hamid had already told her that the heli-pilot was waiting to fly her to the airport. She would not allow herself to drag out their final meeting. Giannis had made her weak, but she was determined to be strong and make a dignified exit.

'You did not give me the wrong impression,' Giannis asserted, his accent very thick. 'I saw you and the deed was done. The hunter's instinct is a powerful one, and the more you resisted me, the more I desired you. I am sorry that I hurt you. But think long and hard before you turn your back on what we share. That happiness is not easily found.'

'But it was fool's gold,' she responded, with a bitterness she had to battle to conceal. 'And it turned to dross in the light of day.'

Dark golden eyes bleak, Giannis watched the helicopter take off. His big, powerful frame taut with frustration, he tossed back a brandy. His stubborn jawline clenched. Her departure had unleashed uncomfortable reactions within him. His resistance to her climbed in direct proportion to that disturbing knowledge, because he disliked the sense that he was not fully in control. Perhaps it was fortunate that he would not see her for a while. After all, he was not a hero, and he had never suffered from the delusion that he might be. He thought it was just typical of Madeleine Conway that she only wanted a guy who was a bloody hero!

She had storybook ideals—fantasy expectations. His conscience, never the most active part of his psyche, creaked into action to remind him that she had believed he was single and unattached. He remembered how gutted she had been. He had behaved like a bastard, he acknowledged unwillingly. He had taken sexual advantage of a starry-eyed virgin who had evidently seen him in much the same light as an infatuated teenager. He recalled the shine in Maddie's eyes when she'd looked at him that first day in his office. He wondered exactly what he would have to do to bring that shine back, and he did not doubt his ability to achieve that end. How was it his fault that other women had asked so little from him that he had become spoilt? Even a little lazy and arrogant?

While Maddie had values that he admired—even if living

with them was a distinct challenge for him—she also had a lot to learn. Krista was not a negotiable element in his life, he reasoned. He had chosen Krista to be his wife, and he was not a changeable man. The only vacancy available was that of mistress. There were strict boundaries between his public life and that which he led in private. Maddie would have to understand and accept it. He would give her the chance to adjust to the concept of compromise. He refused to consider what he would do if she proved stubborn.

After a lengthy delay at the airport, Maddie returned to London and a grey wet morning. She felt the loss of bright sunlight almost as much as the loss of Giannis. He'd had her flown back to London on a Petrakos jet and, mindful of the crew, she had felt obliged to stay dry-eyed. Nemos had carried her bag right to the door of her bedsit, and even put the key in the lock for her. When the door had shut behind her she'd thought how hopelessly dark and drab her rented room seemed.

She was quick to remind herself that this was her real world. Had she resisted temptation, as all her instincts had urged, she would not be feeling as though someone had forcibly torn her in two.

But at least she now understood why her time in Morocco had felt unreal. How could it have felt like anything more serious or durable? Her love affair had just been a casual sexual intrigue to a Greek billionaire for whom one woman was clearly never going to be enough. He had picked her because she had been so amazingly free with her favours in his office. Had she paused to ask him then if he was a single man? No, she had not. So it would be hypocritical to blame him for the entire débâcle. Having torn up the rulebook of how she lived her life, it seemed she was now paying the price for being free and easy.

The next day she was wakened by the delivery of a magnificent bouquet. She would not allow herself to read the card and, although the waste of such beauty brought tears to her eyes, she dumped the flowers.

Feed a cold and starve a fever, her grandmother had often said, and Maddie knew she had a fever that required brutal discouragement. She refused to wallow in the belief that she loved Giannis. How could she have loved someone she hardly knew? She had to get over him and do it quickly. But the craving for him nagged at her like a constant pain. She did not know how to kill the terrible bone-deep longing just to see his lean, dark face one more time. Her peace of mind was gone as well. How would she ever forgive herself for the mistakes she had made? The mistakes she had then excused so that she could go on making them with him? Her self-esteem was at rock bottom.

Keen to get back to work, and even more eager to earn some money, she had already let the employment agency know that she was available again. Luckily she had to work at the supermarket that night. At the end of her shift she emerged wearily for the walk home.

A limo pulled in ahead of her, the chauffeur stepping out to open the passenger door for her. 'Please go away!' she hissed, praying that none of her co-workers were behind her.

But the limo followed her home, and she was on the stairs when Nemos appeared, carrying a large wicker hamper. 'Nemos…please,' she muttered tiredly. 'I don't want this.'

He set the hamper down at her door. 'Mr Petrakos sent us to pick you up from the store and deliver this.'

'Is he still in Morocco?' she heard herself ask.

'Athens…on business.'

Maddie went red, because she knew she wasn't practising what she had preached to Giannis or herself. She shouldn't have asked; where Giannis was and what he might be doing was nothing to do with her any more. At her urging, Nemos took the hamper away again.

She slept badly that night, and woke up at dawn. The smell of someone frying food had drifted into her room and curdled her tummy. Her period was due today, and she was desperate to have her fears set to rest. Might stress and a guilty conscience have made her imagine that she felt dizzy and sick? She was pleased when the agency phoned and told her that she would be temping for the week in a big insurance company. And then her neighbour, Mrs Evans's daughter, asked if Maddie could spend a couple of hours with her mother while she went out. Glad of a distraction from her worries, Maddie went downstairs to sit with the old lady.

Mrs Evans enjoyed the benefit of cable television, and told Maddie to pick a programme from a multitude of channels. Skimming through the many options in the magazine she had been handed, Maddie stiffened in surprise when she saw a photo of Giannis above a few lines about a documentary on his love-life. The programme had already started, but she put it on in time to see an incredibly beautiful blonde girl stepping on board a giant white yacht. From that moment Maddie was hooked, and yet nothing had ever hurt her more than watching that programme.

She made tea for Mrs Evans at a run during the commercial break, so that she didn't miss anything. She was so ashamed of her painful curiosity to know who Krista was, and what she found out only wounded her more.

Set next to Krista Spyridou, with her platinum hair and supermodel looks and gloss, Maddie could only see herself as a plain Jane with a weight problem. She marvelled that the exquisite Krista was not enough to satisfy Giannis. Was he just a rat in the fidelity stakes? Perpetually addicted to the novelty of fresh faces? It was no consolation to see innumerable shots of him with an endless procession of gorgeous high-profile women. But as Maddie watched, learning that Giannis had known Krista since childhood and seeing pictures of them together overlaid with a commentary about how much the couple shared, her heart twisted inside her. They *did* look like a perfectly matched couple. Both of them were Greek, beautiful, rich, sophisticated and fashionable. Maddie knew that she was none of those things, and she wondered how she had contrived to tempt Giannis. Although it hurt her to acknowledge it, she also accepted that Giannis had to genuinely care about Krista. Why else would a guy with so much choice and so much experience have decided to marry her?

As soon as Maddie had finished work the following day, she went straight to a pharmacy and bought a pregnancy testing kit. Her nerves worn thin, she sat in her bedsit and read the instructions over and over until she knew them by heart. When she could no longer put off the moment of truth, she did the test and the result came through very quickly.

She was going to have a baby.

Right on cue she felt light-headed again. She was in shock. In spite of Giannis's immovable belief that there would be no repercussions from the condom accident, she was pregnant. Yet he had almost managed to convince her that she was worrying needlessly. Had that been his wishful thinking? A sob

*Peel off seal and
place inside...*

LIFT
HERE

An Important Message
from the Editors

Dear Reader,

If you'd enjoy reading romance novels with
larger print that's easier on your eyes,
let us send you **TWO FREE HARLEQUIN
PRESENTS® NOVELS** in our **LARGER
PRINT EDITION.** These books are complete
and unabridged, but the type is bigger to
make it easier to read. Look inside for an
actual size sample.

By the way, you'll also get **two surprise
gifts** with your **two free books!**

Pam Powers

84

she'd thought she was fine. It took Daniel's words and Brooke's question to make her realize she was far from a full recovery.

She'd made a start with her sister's help and she intended to go forward now. Sarah felt as if she'd been living in a darkened room and some- one had suddenly opened a door, letting in the fresh air and sunshine. She could feel its warmth slowly seeping into the coldest part of her. The feeling was liberating. She realized it was only a small step and she had a long way to go, but she was ready to face life again with Serena and her family behind her.

All too soon, they were saying goodbye and Sarah experienced a moment of sadness for all the years she and Serena had missed. But they had each other now, and that's what

She held

PRINTED IN THE U.S.A.   © 2006 HARLEQUIN ENTERPRISES LT
® and ™ are trademarks owned and used by the trademark owner and/or its licensee.
Publisher acknowledges the copyright holder of the excerpt from this individual work as follow
THE RIGHT WOMAN Copyright © 2004 by Linda Warren. All rights reserved.

The Harlequin Reader Service® — Here's How it Works:

Accepting your 2 free Harlequin Presents® larger print books and 2 free gifts places you under no obligation to buy anything. You may keep the books and gifts and return the shipping statement marked "cancel". If you do not cancel, about a month later we'll send you 6 additional Harlequin Presents® larger print books and bill you just $4.05 each in the U.S. or $4.72 each in Canada, plus 25¢ shipping & handling per book and applicable taxes if any.* That's the complete price and – compared to cover prices of $4.75 each in the U.S. and $5.75 each in Canada – it's quite a bargain! You may cancel at any time, but if you choose to continue, every month we'll send you 6 more books, which you may either purchase at the discount price or return to us and cancel your subscription.

*Terms and prices subject to change without notice. Sales tax applicable in N.Y. Canadian residents will be charged applicable provincial taxes and GST. Offer limited to one per household. All orders subject to approval. Books received may vary. Credit or debit balances in a customer's account(s) may be offset by any other outstanding balance owed by or to the customer. Please allow 4 to 6 weeks for delivery.

If offer card is missing write to: Harlequin Reader Service, 3010 Walden Ave., P.O. Box 1867, Buffalo, NY 14240-1867

HARLEQUIN READER SERVICE
3010 WALDEN AVE
PO BOX 1867
BUFFALO NY 14240-9952

BUSINESS REPLY MAIL
FIRST-CLASS MAIL   PERMIT NO. 717-003   BUFFALO, NY

POSTAGE WILL BE PAID BY ADDRESSEE

NO POSTAGE
NECESSARY
IF MAILED
IN THE
UNITED STATES

convulsed her throat. Suddenly she felt very young and very scared. She had managed to do everything wrong. She had conceived during a casual sexual encounter. Giannis Petrakos cared nothing for her and would certainly not want her to have his baby. Nor, quite naturally, would Krista Spyridou. What would such news do to Giannis's intended bride?

Maddie wept long and hard with guilt and unhappiness. She knew how gutted *she* would feel if the man she was about to marry got another woman pregnant. Krista, who was innocent of all blame, would be hurt and humiliated. It might also be a very public humiliation, Maddie conceded sickly. Until she had glimpsed the Petrakos lifestyle on television she had really not appreciated just how newsworthy and wealthy Giannis was. If the press were to discover that he had fathered a child by a lowly office temp, the story would almost certainly be front-page news. And what role would be assigned to Maddie in such an unlikely triangle? Most probably that of gold-digging tramp, she reckoned painfully. For she was not a beautiful pedigreed golden girl like his photogenic bride-to-be.

And what good would such a scandal do any one of them? Particularly her poor child, who would have to look back on it all some day in the future? When the contraception had failed Giannis had compared the risk of pregnancy to a disaster. And, unless she was very much mistaken, he had made no further reference to that possibility precisely because it *was* his worst-case scenario come true. In all likelihood he would hope that Maddie would agree to a termination—but she was not prepared to consider that option.

A wave of bitter pain and regret scythed through Maddie. Was it really her duty to pin a chance pregnancy on a man who didn't want to know? A man planning to marry the gorgeous

Krista Spyridou? Hadn't Giannis Petrakos trampled enough on her pride? Did she really have to lower herself to that extent?

So tired that she felt as though she was sleepwalking, Maddie went back into work at the insurance company again the next day. She got wet walking from the bus stop, and shivered in her damp skirt and shoes while she sorted through ancient dusty filing cabinets in a cold, grim basement room. Every few minutes she would remember afresh that she was pregnant, and she would start fretting again.

How would she live? She barely earned enough to feed herself as it was. Babies needed a lot of equipment and clothing. Childcare was very expensive. How would she hold down a job? And if she couldn't manage to stay in employment the baby would not have much of a future to look forward to because they would be living on the poverty line.

Mid-morning, she was called to an office on the ground floor and asked to wait there by a senior manager, who seemed rather nervous and uncomfortable. While she was worried that she had done something wrong, she was grateful to have the chance to sit down in comparative warmth and comfort.

When the door opened, she rose to her feet in an uncertain motion. An almost inaudible gasp parted her lips when Giannis appeared.

'What are you doing here?' Maddie shook her bright head in disbelief.

CHAPTER SIX

GIANNIS ran brilliant dark golden eyes over Maddie's pale, shaken face. He was disconcerted by the change in her. She had bluish-grey shadows below her eyes, and the triangular fragility of her face had taken on a pinched quality that suggested she had lost weight in only the few days since he'd last seen her. His black brows drew together in a frown.

'You look terrible.'

Pained colour seared her cheeks. No, she had no inner glow like his very beautiful fiancée—no glistening straight blonde hair, no thinner-than-thin perfect body to offer. Of course he must have seen Krista again while he was in Greece. Of course he was now comparing her to Krista, possibly without even knowing he was doing it. Her already laden conscience urged her to stifle such inappropriate thoughts. She was jealous, downright horribly jealous, of a woman she had wronged! The shame of that awareness cut through her, and she hated Giannis for bringing her down to such a level.

'Are you ill?' Giannis demanded.

'No, of course I'm not!' Maddie spun away, turning her back on him while she struggled to rescue her composure.

In her mind's eye she could still see him, and her heart was racing and pounding as if she had run up a hill. One glimpse of his lean, darkly handsome face, one scorching encounter with his gilded bronze eyes, and she wanted to throw herself at him. For a split second, a wicked moment in time, it didn't matter what he had done. She just wanted to forgive him so that she could be with him again. The coiled knot of heat in her pelvis was radiating a wanton physical awareness that shook her. Her breasts were heavy, the rosy tips swollen.

Affronted by her weakness, she forced herself to concentrate, and turned back to him. 'What are you doing here? How did you manage to walk into this office?' she asked in an accusing rush. 'How did you even know where I was?'

'I own this company.' Giannis spread long brown fingers in a stylish gesture of dismissal. 'I wanted a meeting, and it was arranged with discretion.'

'You actually *own* this business?' Maddie prompted, half an octave higher. 'Is that why I was offered the chance to work here this week?'

'If you must work—and I would prefer that you did *not,*' Giannis murmured with silken stress, 'why not work for me?'

'Why? Does it give you a kick, pushing people around? Like I'm some piece on a chessboard and this is a game?'

His keen gaze narrowed and glittered. 'I want you back, *pedhi mou.* I very much regret the distress I have caused. This is definitely not a game for either of us.'

'And would you still feel the same way if I was pregnant?' Maddie heard herself throwing that provocative challenge, and was startled by her daring. She was toying with the truth that she was not yet ready to voice, testing the water. But the instant she finished speaking she realised that now she would have to tell him she had conceived.

The answering silence yawned like a frightening abyss. Her fingers clenched into her palms and etched little purple crescents. She wanted—no, *needed* a positive response. All her hopes were laid out in a pathetic line in front of her, vulnerable and defenceless.

His lean, strong face had shuttered. His beautiful smart dark eyes, semi-screened by his dense black lashes, narrowed to grim points of light. '*Are* you pregnant?'

That single demand came with the telling speed and precision of a bullet to the heart. The chill factor in the air turned her to pure ice, and pain threatened to crack her down the middle. 'No,' she heard herself say cheerfully, hiding her true feelings behind all the pride she could muster.

Only ferocious self-discipline prevented Giannis from swearing out loud. What a question to throw at him! His perfect white teeth were gritted. The fall-out from such a development would rock the foundations of his world. Why the hell had she asked him that? What a stupid, tasteless question! As if a pregnancy could be anything other than a major catastrophe that would require handling. Babies and mistresses didn't go together.

Maddie hated him at that moment. She wanted to wrap her arms protectively round her still-flat stomach. She wanted to shout that her baby would do just fine with her, and would never, ever need a selfish and heartless rat like him as an uninterested father. Instead she said flatly, 'I'd like to go back to work. Please don't approach me again.'

'How long are you planning to keep this up?' Giannis growled with furious impatience and growing frustration. Once again she was behaving differently from all the other women who had preceded her. 'I won't be back in London for at least two weeks.'

A humourless little laugh escaped Maddie. 'Why are you telling me that? Didn't you hear me? I'm asking you to leave me alone.'

Before she would work out his intention, Giannis strode forward, closed his hands over hers and claimed her luscious mouth with a devouring, driving heat that left her giddy and breathless. 'Let's not talk,' he breathed in a heartfelt plea. 'Let's go back to my apartment.'

Maddie peeled herself off him again. It was quite an operation: she was leaning into him, with her fingers clenched on his shoulder, her other hand splayed across his shirt-front, her palm warmed by his body heat and the steady thump of his heartbeat. Another few seconds and she knew she would have been inside his jacket with him. No wonder he was inviting her back to his apartment. She was a slut—a total slut, she told herself in disgust. That one passionate kiss had set up a chain reaction of craving that made her entire body melt and quiver.

'No. I—'

Giannis curved long fingers round her wrist to halt her steady retreat towards the door. 'What do you want me to do? Beg?' he ground out.

With a mighty effort of will, Maddie yanked her fingers free and stepped back from him. 'You're engaged—'

'That's business… You're very much in the pleasure category,' Giannis murmured in a roughened undertone.

Her green eyes glinted pure emerald, and defiance was written in every rigid line of her shapely figure and stance. 'But I don't want to be with you now. You're wrong for me.'

'There aren't many old-style heroes out there.' His golden eyes challenged her.

Maddie was trembling. 'Perhaps not…but I'm sure there are a few decent, trustworthy guys left. Maybe even one with principles, who doesn't think his money entitles him to do as he likes. Some day I'll meet someone I can respect—and, believe me, he's not you!'

His face saturnine in cast, Giannis had fallen very still, for he was not accustomed to being insulted. A forbidding light had entered his piercing dark eyes. 'Regardless of what it takes, you will learn to respect me. I can wait. I will be patient. In the end I always get what I want.'

'But I won't ever be with you again,' Maddie vowed vehemently. 'Now I'm going back to work.'

She returned to the filing room in the basement. For several minutes she stared into space and tried to still the inner trembling affecting her. She felt cold inside and out, and utterly bereft. Hating him and wanting him was threatening to tear her apart. But now there was a kernel of fear edging her responses. For how long would she be able to withstand the dangerous combination of his strength and determination pitted against her own longing?

Sensible people moved on from mistakes, and perhaps she needed to move on in a literal sense, she reasoned feverishly. She had no ties in London, and it was a very expensive place to live. If she moved away now she would be able to make a fresh start well in advance of her baby's birth. If Giannis did not know where she was he would have to leave her alone, and she would not be tempted back into a relationship that would destroy her. While she might have little money in her bank account, she did have a post office savings nest-egg which contained the fifteen hundred pounds that her grandmother had left her. It would cover the expense of any move.

That evening, Maddie began going through her things and sorting out what could be recycled through a charity shop and what should have been dumped long ago. Travelling light would make relocating less of a challenge.

And would you still feel the same way if I was pregnant?

The ultimate high jump, Giannis conceded in vexation, an austere cast to his wide handsome mouth. It had been a test, however, and he had failed it. Until he had met Madeleine Conway, Giannis had believed that a luxurious lifestyle and extravagant gifts were sufficient to tempt any woman into pleasing him. But Maddie was complex, challenging, and yet in many ways more basic. What did Stone Age Woman want from Stone Age Man? Giannis asked himself grimly. Stone Age Woman expected her guy to supply protection, food and shelter. In much the same way, Maddie wanted a guy she could depend on to look after her in all circumstances. So she had thrown the pregnancy loop and he had bombed. Why? Like most very rich men, he was accustomed to dealing with avaricious scheming women and ceding nothing, calling in his lawyers to clean up and ensure that the press never got wind of it.

Maddie, however, had been asking a simple question to establish the level of his commitment to her. *What if?* And, cynical, guarded and astute as he was, he had been too clever for his own good. She had expected an honest response, but he could not recall when he had ever answered a leading question from a woman with simple candour. He avoided relationship discussions. He dumped women prone to striking up such conversations. But Maddie occupied a class of her own, and she required more painstaking management and support. She had needed to hear that, whatever happened, he would take care of her. Regrettably, she had given him insufficient time to work out the reality that only forthright sincerity would win him a hearing.

'Mr Petrakos…?' one of the Greek board members murmured. For the silence had lasted and lasted, and everyone round the massive table was getting very nervous.

Giannis shot him a chilling glance. 'Don't interrupt me. I'm thinking.'

What the hell had Maddie been playing at? Giannis wondered in seething frustration. Where did she get the nerve to tell him that he was not decent, honourable or worthy of respect? Surely only the most severe distress could have provoked her into such base accusations? She should have had the sense to appreciate that a guy with as much money as he had could not possibly afford to ignore or deny the potential time-bomb that would arise from the existence of an illegitimate child. Just because he had never felt any great need to reproduce it did not mean he did not know what was right and proper, either. Some day, after all, he might have children with Krista.

Without warning he was assailed by the image of a spoilt, imperious little girl with a bored, petulant expression, who only cracked a smile when she looked in the mirror. It was closely followed by an equally daunting image of an ignorant, idle son with the same sulky vacant look that Krista wore when the conversation went above her head. If her genes triumphed, what would happen to the Petrakos power-base in the next generation? Giannis was unable to repress a shudder. At that precise moment he knew that he would not marry Krista. He could not work out how he had ever believed that he could.

* * *

Forty-eight hours later, Giannis flew out to Paris to break off his engagement. Since their betrothal Krista had been using all his properties, and was currently staying in his townhouse there while she visited friends. He did not give advance warning of his arrival, and when he strode into the hall Krista was screaming like a virago at a cowering maid.

'Giannis…' Tiny spots of colour adorning her perfect cheekbones, Krista dismissed the tear-stained member of staff with an imperious wave and turned to greet him as though nothing had happened.

'Problems?' Giannis enquired.

Krista complained that he was so rare a visitor to the household that his staff had become sloppy. Giannis was sceptical, because he had seen the vicious look etched on Krista's face. He had once heard a rumour that the Spyridous had paid off a maid who'd accused Krista of assault. His fiancée gave him a winsome smile that displayed her pearly teeth to perfection. It was wasted on Giannis, who had not only been put in mind of his late mother's drug-fuelled tirades against her long-suffering servants, but who had also remembered Maddie's unfailing courtesy with his staff in Morocco. Impatient, however, to do what had to be done, he said nothing more on the subject. In the huge, airy drawing room, he told Krista as gently as he could that he no longer wanted to marry her.

'You don't mean it… It's the wedding arrangements giving you cold feet,' Krista informed him.

'The fault is mine. I'm not ready to make such a commitment,' Giannis countered steadily.

'But you won't find being married to me any different to

being single!' Krista pouted. 'Giannis…I know you enjoy your freedom. You're a Petrakos male. Womanising is in your blood.'

'I'm sorry. Our engagement is at an end.'

'But I've made so many arrangements.'

Giannis was quick to assure her that his staff would take care of everything. He was prepared for her every protest. Like a rock in a storm, he withstood reproaches, thwarted tears of rage and a screaming tantrum. Her greatest source of concern was that she would look foolish, and she baulked at his suggestion that they release an immediate joint statement to the press. In a rare gesture he agreed to let her choose the timing and the content of any such announcement.

Also, because he did feel that his change of heart was very hard on her, Giannis presented her with a jewellery case. He had purchased the contents as a wedding gift. 'Please accept this set as a token of my continuing affection and esteem.'

Krista was as responsive to the glimpse of a large jewel case as a well-trained snake was to a charmer. The magnificent diamond and sapphire set, once the property of now deposed European royalty, brought ecstatic gasps of delight to her lips. Suddenly she was all smiles again.

Giannis was leaving when she said brightly, 'I'll wait for you to get this bug out of your system.'

He sent her a wry glance. 'It's not a bug.'

She tossed her hair so that it fell like pale blonde candy floss round her exquisite face. 'I'm perfect for you. Everybody says so. When we get back together we'll be like Romeo and Juliet.'

'It's over, Krista.' Giannis resisted the urge to point out how Romeo and Juliet's romance had ended. Instead he rejoiced in the energising sense of freedom gripping him. He knew he would never propose marriage again. It had been a serious mistake on his part. He should have listened to his instincts. If he needed a hostess he would hire one. Maddie had held a mirror up to him, and he did not like the reflection he'd seen.

Thirty-six hours after attending business talks in Dubai, Giannis flew back to London. Although he had yet to forgive Maddie's behaviour at their last meeting, he could not wait to see her, and he went straight to her bedsit, planning to surprise her.

But the surprise was his, because there was no answer at her door. By the next day Nemos had established that she had moved out of her accommodation without leaving a forwarding address. Giannis insisted on seeing the room and having it searched. He could not credit that she was gone.

Why? He was a very logical guy. But he still could not comprehend why. No woman had ever run away from him before. Why would she do that? She wanted him as much as he wanted her. What was her problem? One minute she kissed him as if she couldn't live without him, and the *next*— Raging frustration sizzled through his big, powerful frame. How long would it take him to track her down? There was a chance that he might never find her. That was the cue for the weirdest sense of paralysis setting in to his long powerful legs. Aggressively healthy as he was, he wondered if he was coming down with an illness.

Only when he had swung back into the limo did Nemos bend down to pass him an item. 'It was in the rubbish bin. I thought you'd want me to be discreet.'

It was the packaging for a pregnancy testing kit. So evidently she had been worried—much more worried than he had been, Giannis registered in surprise. Had he struck her as insensitive? He grimaced. Why was that word working its way into his vocabulary? He had simply thought it improbable that the only contraceptive failure he had ever experienced would lead to conception. And he had been proven right, hadn't he? But at least he now understood why she had been so angry when they'd last met. She had resented his more mature outlook and his calm lack of concern on that score—which now he found perfectly understandable.

The magazine was well read, and its cover was beginning to come off. Even from the other side of the waiting room, however, Maddie recognised the juxtaposed photos of Giannis and Krista. Practically in one motion, she pushed herself up off her seat and swept the publication off the table. The issue was weeks old. On the cover, a jagged lightening flash split a photo of the couple apart, and below ran the headline: *Jilted?* Too impatient to sit down again, she stood flicking through the pages in search of the corresponding article. It took several minutes for her to find it, because the piece was only a few lines long and not very informative.

An unnamed mutual 'friend' had let it be known that the Greek society wedding of the year was off. No reasons were given. Both Giannis and Krista had refused to comment on the rumours, and had asked for their privacy to be respected. Maddie drew in a slow, deep breath and clutched the magazine tightly.

'Miss Conway?'

'And this is your *first* visit to us?' The middle-aged doctor sighed as he weighed her and took her blood pressure. 'You must be at least five months pregnant.'

'About four months…' Maddie told him. 'I saw a doctor in Southend when I was about six weeks along. Everything was fine then.'

The doctor said nothing. Unless she was mistaken about the dates, he thought, there was a problem. She was very noticeably pregnant. She looked thin and tired, and he wasn't happy with her blood pressure. He examined her and said that he would like her to have a scan at the hospital.

'Also, I don't think you should be working,' he added.

'I'm only doing a few hours here and there. I can't afford to quit.'

'Do you want this baby?'

Losing what little colour she had, Maddie nodded in dismay.

'Then you need to rest and take it easy.'

Fear gripped Maddie. The only thing that had kept her sane through the long lonely weeks since she had left London had been the comforting prospect of her child. True, she had felt endlessly tired, and sick enough to lose her appetite and some weight, but it had not occurred to her that her pregnancy might be at risk. Confronted with that threat, she was appalled. She was living in a bed-and-breakfast, and working odd shifts as a cashier in a restaurant which was open to all hours.

But if Giannis was no longer engaged there was no reason why she shouldn't contact him and ask him to help her out. Naturally she would have preferred to remain proudly independent—not least because she had not told him the truth when she might have done. But all of a sudden she was painfully and guiltily aware that she should be putting her baby first and her pride and her feelings last.

It was months since Giannis had given her the embossed business card, but she still had it in her purse. Before she could lose her momentum, she went into the shopping centre to find a public phone. She punched out his mobile number very slowly. Her heart was beating so fast and her mind was so full of apprehensive thoughts that she very nearly dropped the receiver before the call was answered.

Giannis spoke in Greek, which unnerved her.

'Hello…it's me,' she announced stiltedly. 'I mean, sorry…it's Maddie.'

At the other end of the phone, Giannis rose from his seat. Every predatory instinct on instant hyper-alert, he murmured as smoothly as silk, 'I've been hoping to hear from you. Where are you?'

The rich, accented timbre of his deep voice touched memories Maddie had not known she had, and brought a surge of unexpected moisture to her eyes. 'I'm in Reading,' she said gruffly. 'I need to see you.'

'Any time. Give me your address—I'll send a car to pick you up,' Giannis suggested, determined to pin her down to an exact geographical location.

Not yet ready to advance that amount of trust, Maddie spread uneasy fingers over the gentle swell of her stomach. 'No. I'll get the train to London this afternoon.'

An expert negotiator, Giannis knew when not to push. He had picked up on that audible note of wariness. 'Where do you want to meet? My apartment?'

'No…' But her mind, she discovered, was a total blank. The doctor had said it was hormones, but sometimes she felt as if her brain had been hijacked.

She had no objection, therefore, to Giannis stepping straight into the breach with the immediate assurance that she would be met at the station and brought to a hotel where they could dine.

'It'll be very relaxed.' Giannis was determined to do and say whatever it took to draw her out of hiding, though he was using persuasive tactics that were utterly new to him.

Maddie wondered dully how hungry he would feel after she had broken her news. Since she could hardly take care of that in a public restaurant, she felt she had to say in warning, 'I sort of need to talk to you in private.'

Whatever, Giannis thought, energised by a wave of satisfaction and impatience. She had missed him. Of course she had. He had picked up on a hint of tears in her voice, but even so she had stayed away for over three bloody months! Strange how a woman who could be so gentle could also be as stubborn as a mule and as hard as granite. He realised that he was as angry with her as he was pleased, and it was a volatile combination. But stronger than either prompting ran a deep, atavistic need to stamp her as his again, with the raw, physical intimacy that would ensure she never ran in the wrong direction again. This enthralling imagery in mind, Giannis cancelled all his afternoon appointments with a casualness that shocked his personal assistants.

Even though it was a hot day, Maddie wore a long jacket which, amazingly, did a good job of concealing her changing shape. Nemos greeted her with a warm, welcoming smile and shepherded her through the busy station. She alighted in a quiet side street. The lavish hotel foyer was wrapped in the intimidating silence of an exclusive establishment. Her nervous tension increased, her palms dampening.

'Mr Petrakos is in here…' A door was spread back and she saw him for herself: tall, vibrantly dark and devastatingly handsome, he wore a silver-grey business suit with the classy sheen of madly expensive silk. He was *all* she saw—the only element in the room that she could focus on. A tiny pulse was beating too fast in the hollow of her collarbone.

His first thought was that she looked incredibly lovely, like a painting brought to life. She looked tiny and fragile in a voluminous black jacket which acted as a vivid foil for her Titian mane of curls and pure white skin.

'Would you like a drink?' he murmured softly.

'Oh, no—I mean…'

Giannis strode forward and offered to take her coat. He didn't like the way she was hovering, or the evasiveness of her green eyes. He had never been so tense. He was trying not to think of what he would do if she decided to walk away again.

'No…no, it's okay.' Maddie backed away, and then thought how ridiculous she must look—how pointless it was for her to try and delay the announcement that she had to make. 'I've got something to tell you.'

'You're very jumpy? I can see that for myself.'

Maddie breathed in deep. 'About three months ago I told you a lie.'

'You're forgiven,' Giannis asserted huskily, feasting his appreciative and somewhat amused gaze on her, because he was convinced that what she termed a lie would only qualify as the most minor fib. After all, nobody knew better than he did that she had sterling principles set in stone.

'But you don't know what I lied about yet.'

His gilded bronze eyes narrowed and raked over her, lingering on the soft pink fullness of her mouth. 'You look amazing. You'd have to be a guy to understand. Promise to come home with me tonight and I won't even ask what the lie was, *pedhi mou.*'

Maddie could not initially credit his response, and then intimate and deeply embarrassing memories stirred and surfaced. He exuded hot, sexual energy, and he had taught her the meaning of exquisite pleasure. A heavy flush heated her entire skin surface. She could not deny that in Morocco she had been with him every step of the way. Furthermore, the extent of the passion he'd awakened had shocked her. She had not even known that it was possible for her to want a man to the extent that he could make her want him. So was it any wonder that he did not take her very seriously?

'Do you ever think of anything other than the bedroom stuff?' she asked in a stifled tone of discomfiture.

'Not around you…it colours everything,' Giannis confided in a driven undertone, opting for the honesty that she had insisted she wanted from him. 'It even gets in the way of business. Perhaps if I had you all to myself for an unspecified length of time, and I could live out my every erotic desire, I could think of other things…occasionally.'

'Like…as in having a serious conversation?' Maddie prompted tightly, as she unbuttoned her jacket with trembling hands.

'Don't hold your breath, *glikia mou.*' His lean, strong face taut, his brilliant dark eyes flashed languorous gold above his bronzed cheekbones. 'I'm not into those.'

Maddie yanked off her jacket in a decidedly challenging fashion and pitched it at a chair, fearful that at any moment she would lose her nerve. She also hated herself for the fact that she really didn't want to show him her pregnant body. He had found her *unpregnant* body deeply attractive and sensual.

'And possibly you aren't either,' Giannis added thickly, hoping very much that she was going to continue with the strip.

He didn't care how many serious conversations he had to be subjected to afterwards. Indeed, he dimly accepted that that might well be the price. She was a little conscience on legs, heavily prone to feeling bad about his natural human flaws. He just wished she could see how simple everything would be if she could only think as he did. She was back. They were together. He wanted her to come home with him. What was wrong with a celebration? There was no need to discuss the fact that she now had her own discreet surveillance team of three, who would ensure that she never got lost again. No, he didn't make the same mistake twice.

'G-Giannis…?' Maddie stammered, the tip of her tongue sliding out to moisten her lower lip in the heavy silence. She had assumed that he would immediately notice that her trim waist had vanished.

Instead his smouldering gaze was locked to the sinfully ripe contours of her moist pink lips. 'I love your mouth…'

Maddie realised that her black T-shirt and stretchy skirt were doing a better job of concealment than she had expected. Sucking in her breath, in the pathetic hope that some of her tummy would go in with it, she muttered unevenly, 'Don't you notice anything?'

On an erotic high of anticipation, Giannis was taking his time about inspecting her wonderfully rounded shape. The voluptuous curve of her bosom left him spellbound, and his scrutiny lingered there with the purist's attention to detail. He was picturing her on his bed, in his office, in his apartment, on his private jet. Always there for him, always available. 'Your breasts are amazing…'

Maddie went scarlet with rage and stress and disbelief and turned sideways. 'What about my stomach?'

Sleek ebony brows pleating, Giannis stared. Black lashes lowering, he blinked, too taken aback to instantly grasp why she should look from that angle as if she had swallowed a cushion. 'Enormous…'

Her eyes smarted; her face tightened and paled. Well, he had shot straight from the hip—and she had always known that he would find her rotund proportions deeply unappealing, hadn't she?

'Pregnant,' Giannis almost whispered in Greek. And then he said it again for good measure in English. 'But you can't be pregnant because you said you were not.'

A silence full of dangerous sparks began to simmer in the tense atmosphere.

'Isn't that so?' Giannis murmured lethally.

CHAPTER SEVEN

MADDIE winced at that direct hit. 'Yes, but—'

Giannis focused on her with a fierce intensity that made her feel horribly like a condemned prisoner in the dock. 'Is this the lie you mentioned?'

Maddie nodded reluctant confirmation.

Giannis lifted a strong hand and brought it down again in a compelling motion. A warning flare of gold was glimmering in his gaze. 'You are not forgiven.'

'I realise that this is a shock for you…'

Outrage was roaring through Giannis, who prided himself on his control of his temper. It was bad enough that she had disappeared, but that she should have done so when she carried his child incensed him. All those wasted months when they might have been together. 'It is a great deal more than a shock—'

Coppery red curls streamed back from her oval face as her chin came up. 'A disaster? That *is* how you labelled the possibility of me conceiving.'

'That is unjust. You're rewinding right back to the first day we met to quote a casual comment?' Giannis shot back at her, fast as the speed of light.

'What was casual about it? It wasn't casual for me,' Maddie

protested painfully. 'I may not have known it that day, but you were engaged. Yes, I accept that it was casual for you, and of course you didn't want me to have your child. Why can't you just admit that me falling pregnant is the worst situation you can imagine?'

His lean, darkly handsome face hardened. 'Do not tell me how I think or how I feel,' he intoned in sizzling disdain. 'Don't make excuses for yourself either!'

Maddie dealt him a defensive glance. 'I'm not—'

'You are—and it makes what you have done even more unacceptable. So I didn't think you would conceive?' Giannis flung up his hands and contrived to shrug his indifference to that angle of argument. His Greek heritage had never been more apparent to her. 'But you *did* conceive and the instant that occurred everything changed for both of us.'

'How?' Maddie realised that she had very much underestimated the depth of his anger.

Stunning eyes fiercely intent, Giannis studied her. He moved away a little to get a better view. The lush mound of her once flat stomach was fast becoming a source of fascination to him. He could not recall ever looking at a pregnant woman before. He had not had the slightest interest. But this was different—*she* was different in that starring role. Somewhere deep within his male psyche a primitive glow of satisfaction burned with his every fresh appraisal of her altered figure. He was fertile. She was carrying *his* seed in her belly.

'The child is mine,' he pointed out. 'From the first moment I had a right to be involved in every decision you made.'

Maddie was squirming, wishing he would stop glancing at her tummy as if he expected her to expand in girth before his very eyes, like Jack's beanstalk. 'That's not how I see it.'

'Then you had better learn to see it my way. Look at what a hash you have already made of things!' Giannis launched in sudden fierce accusation. 'How dare you go away without telling me you were expecting my child? What am I? Such a tyrant that you exclude me from what I should have known from the outset?'

'I have not made a hash of things!' Green eyes bright emerald with defiance, Maddie screwed her hands into fists. 'I thought I was doing you and your fiancée a favour.'

'Nonsense!' Giannis raked back at her with lethal derision. 'You took off without telling me *because* I was engaged. That was my punishment and your revenge—'

'That's an awful thing to accuse me of… As if I'd be so petty and selfish and downright spiteful!'

'The first thing you can do is tell me where you have been all these weeks,' Giannis informed her grimly.

Her brow was tight with tension and she rubbed it with her fingers. 'I moved to Southend, but I had trouble with the landlord so I had to move on again—'

'What sort of trouble?'

Her soft mouth compressed. 'He kept on calling in to see me and it gave me the creeps.'

'I would soon have dealt with him,' Giannis growled, inflamed by that admission. 'Why did you not phone me then?'

'It wasn't any big deal. But…' Maddie worried at her lower lip and sighed unhappily, feeling ashamed that she had not managed the business of surviving more efficiently. 'That second move left me broke, and it was hard to get work. With me in this condition, not every job was suitable either.'

Dragging his smouldering gaze from her, Giannis stood by the window, his tall well-built frame rigid, his broad shoulders straight as an axe handle. He was deeply aggrieved by her failure to approach him for support. Every word she spoke increased his displeasure. No woman had ever denied him his proper place in her life. No woman had ever behaved as though he could not be trusted.

'So what happened to those fine principles of yours?' he derided. 'You were so proud of your ethics. Where were they when you walked away from me without telling me that you had become the mother of my child?'

Maddie shifted uncomfortably. 'I really did think I was doing the best thing—'

'But I listened when you talked about your principles and I trusted you.' Giannis directed a chilling look of censure at her. 'Yet you lied to me—'

'It was an emotional time for me. I was feeling very guilty,' Maddie muttered unhappily. 'But I do see now that if I was involved in the break-up of your engagement then I shouldn't have gone away after I discovered that I was pregnant.'

Giannis stiffened, and his brilliant dark eyes screened to a very wary glitter below his dense black lashes. That particular association of ideas disturbed him. She was moving way too far and too fast for him. 'There was no connection. You played no part in the break-up,' he emphasized, smooth as polished steel. 'I hope that eases your conscience.'

'Yes.'

But Maddie was quite unaware of her conscience at that moment. His sardonic response had struck like a dagger in the heart, and she felt so wounded by his blunt rejection that she did not dare to look at him. From that hurt came a deeper self-knowledge and a horrid sense of humiliation. The instant she had learnt that Giannis and Krista had split up she had grasped the first excuse to contact him and rush back to his side. How revealing was that? How full of herself she must have sounded when she made the assumption that their affair might have led to his change of heart about marrying Krista! She wanted to cringe.

'Don't tell me any more lies. I expect more from you, *pedhi mou*,' Giannis concluded, keenly appraising her small figure again. Even as he looked, his anger at the way she had kept him in the dark steadily receded. Though pregnant, she was gorgeous. He was beginning to adjust to the shock of her new body shape. In fact he was finding her burgeoning figure distinctly pleasing. After all *he*, he acknowledged, was responsible for that change.

Maddie, on the other hand, was feeling more than a little fragile. He had knocked the emotional stuffing out of her. She was just a woman he had slept with who had got in the family way. As she brushed her curls back from her brow, her tummy gave a warning lurch of nausea. She was nothing special to him. Her forehead dampened with perspiration. But he had somehow become so very special to her. Terrified of being sick in his vicinity, she struggled to block that painful passage of thought. She snatched in a discreet gulp of oxygen in an effort to combat the wave of dizziness consuming her and backed blindly down into a seat.

'Giannis, I…' As the giddy attack of nausea worsened, Maddie leapt up again in a sudden movement, intending to leave the room. But darkness folded in on her like a suffocating blanket and she keeled over in a dead faint.

For a split second Giannis just surveyed her in horror. But then he reacted quickly. He hit the alarm on his watch to call his security team, and crouched down beside her to put her in the recovery position.

Maddie swam back to consciousness and loosed a startled moan as a camera flash almost blinded her. 'What...what on earth?'

Mounting the steps to doors already flung wide for their entrance, Giannis tightened his arms round her slight frame. 'Paparazzi,' he growled. 'They were waiting outside the hotel and they followed us here. Blood-sucking vultures!'

'Where are we?'

'A private clinic. I want you checked out.'

'But I saw a doctor this morning,' Maddie argued.

'He didn't do you much good,' Giannis told her forcefully.

'I haven't eaten since breakfast, which was stupid of me,' she groaned. 'Put me down, for goodness' sake. I can walk perfectly well!'

Striking ebony brows accentuating his frown, Giannis lowered her with great care to the floor. But when she tried to stand upright her head started swimming again, and she had to grab at his sleeve to correct her balance.

'All talk and no action,' Giannis censured, scooping her off her feet again. 'Let me do what I do best.'

Maddie was belatedly conscious that other people were around: Nemos and his men, and medical staff. Just about everybody seemed to be staring at them. 'Like bossing people around?' she quipped.

The forbidding tension in his lean bronzed features eased, and he laughed in appreciation. He bent his arrogant dark head and whispered with husky mockery, 'I do a lot of things better than other people, *glikia mou.*'

'Showing off?' Regardless of their audience, she was insanely tempted to wrap her arms round him and hug him tight. She wanted to trap the moment and the memory, so that she could take it out some time in the future, when he was no longer around.

He had taught her how vulnerable she could be. In leaving London she had done what she'd believed was best in a bad situation. But there had not been a day in the intervening weeks when she had not thought of him, missed him, and longed for even just five minutes back in his energising company.

Giannis settled Maddie down on an examination couch in a plush office, and turned to address the consultant gynaecologist who had evidently been awaiting their arrival.

Having banished Giannis, Maddie answered loads of questions. While she was being examined she confided that she thought there was nothing wrong with her aside of tiredness and hunger.

'I can hear two heartbeats,' the consultant told her quietly. 'I'm almost certain you're carrying twins.'

Maddie sucked in a startled breath and then, thinking of her lost twin, Suzy, she slowly began to smile.

Giannis was pacing outside the room when she reappeared, seated in a wheelchair. 'They won't let me walk either. I'll be finished as soon as I have a scan,' she told him apologetically. 'You know…I'm fine.'

'No, I don't know it. That's for the medics to say. I'd like to be present for the scan.'

Maddie acquiesced, because she was feeling a little intimidated by the level of attention she was receiving, not to mention her swanky surroundings. From the minute the doctor urged her to watch the monitor, however, she was entranced by the astonishingly clear images in 3D, delivered by the state-of-the-art ultrasound equipment.

'That's a baby…' Giannis whispered in stark amazement.

He had expected to see very little that was recognizable, and certainly not a tiny face.

'Oh, he's so…so beautiful,' Maddie framed chokily.

Giannis closed a hand over hers. 'Are we having a boy?'

'Do you want to know?'

'Yes, I think I'd like to,' Maddie confessed.

'This one is a boy…'

'You can tell even at this stage?' Giannis was studying the monitor in awe. 'So we are to have a boy. But what did you mean when you said "this one"?'

'I'm having twins,' Maddie told him, suddenly appreciating that she had yet to share that information with him, and feeling sad that she had imposed that division between them.

'It's a little difficult to be sure with the babies in this position, but I'm almost certain the other is a girl,' the consultant added.

'*Theos mou*…twins.' Giannis was stunned, and his lean, shapely hand tightened on hers, his thumb and forefinger gently massaging her wrist. As spellbound as she was, his attention was held by the brilliant clarity of the images.

'Are they healthy?' Maddie pressed anxiously.

The reassurance she received eased her instinctive concern. She was urged to stop worrying, eat more, and get plenty of sleep.

Giannis tucked her back into the wheelchair with great care. He was in a daze. Two children—his son and daughter—his blood. He was astonished by his sense of satisfaction and his even stronger sense of anticipation. He had always believed that he did not care whether he had children or not. But the instant those tiny faces had appeared on the screen something very fundamental had changed in him. Out of his wondering pride had grown a fierce feeling of protectiveness towards Maddie and the babies she carried.

'I'll take you home now. You can eat, just like the doctor ordered, and then rest.'

As Giannis spoke, the limousine pulled away from the rear entrance of the clinic where it had picked them up. She stared out at the camera-wielding paparazzi, pelting in mad frustrated flight round the corner, having realised too late that they had missed their quarry's exit from the clinic.

'My City apartment isn't far from here.'

Her face shadowed, and she closed her hands together on her lap, deliberately not looking at him. 'No, please. That wouldn't be a good idea. I'd rather go to a hotel—'

'Don't be silly,' Giannis interposed in an incredulous tone.

'Hotels are very expensive, but that'll do fine if you can't sort me out with anything else in the short term,' Maddie reasoned doggedly. 'I do need your financial help right now. I'd be grateful if you helped me find more permanent accommodation and made it possible for me to manage on my own.'

'But you're not going to be your own. I've no intention of letting you out of my sight, *pedhi mou*.'

Maddie sent him a sidewise glance and collided unwarily with gilded bronze eyes filled with level enquiry. Her heart seemed to flip inside her chest. Just a glimpse of his lean, darkly handsome face could make her ache with emotion, need, and the most terrible hunger. So she dragged her scrutiny from him again and stared woodenly into space. She had never been sensible with him. In fact she had been stupid, immature and weak. But now that she was pregnant the time for such self-indulgence was past. Her babies needed a mother who behaved like an intelligent adult.

'Giannis…will you listen to me for a moment?' she asked tautly. 'I need to be independent. I wouldn't feel comfortable in your apartment. You slept with me and I fell accidentally pregnant. That's the only reason I'm here with you now. You don't need to pretend that there's anything more.'

Giannis did not like the sound of what he was hearing. She was pulling away from him just when he wanted to manacle her ankle and wrist to his side. 'But there *is* more—'

'No, there isn't.' There was a choky sensation at the foot of Maddie's tight throat, because it would be a long time before she forgot his confident declaration that she had had nothing whatsoever to do with his broken engagement. Yet even if his honesty had hurt she was grateful for it. Her hopes and dreams had tumbled like sandcastles met by the tide. She loved him. She was absolutely hopelessly in love with him. But he didn't feel the same way. She had to learn to live with that reality, and the less time she spent in his vicinity the better.

'Maddie…' Giannis chided, ready to fight bone and sinew until she came round to his point of view. If she didn't stay in his apartment she would be a constant source of worry— for how else was he to know where she was, who she was with, and whether or not she was looking after herself properly?

'I hope you'll take an interest in our children when they're born, and that we can both behave like civilised people,' she muttered feverishly, her eyes hot and scratchy with the tears she was fighting back, that were forcing her to bend her head.

Giannis was about to inform her that a threat to stray with their unborn children away from his care and custody was an act of unjust and warranted aggression which he refused to accept. But then something happened to change his mind. A single drop of moisture splashed down onto her tightly clenched hands. It was a tear. He froze in shock. She rubbed at her eyes and sniffed, murmuring a muffled apology.

'Please don't!' she gasped in dismay, shifting away as though he was contagious when he attempted to put an arm round her.

Giannis was fiercely frustrated by his feeling of power-lessness. She was trembling, clearly distressed, but he was not allowed to hold her or offer comfort. He passed her a pristine linen handkerchief. She mopped up in a no-nonsense way that would have made him smile at any other time. Tears, which he had previously disdained as a base feminine weapon, had a disturbingly strong impact on him when it was Maddie doing the crying. She made him feel like a huge bully. She was tired, unhappy, and pregnant with his children. He did not want to upset her or intimidate her into doing his bidding. For the first time in his life he reined back his strong personality and shelved his arguments along with his impatience. For her sake, he decided to go slowly and take her to a hotel.

The next day Maddie got up after a night of undisturbed slumber. She had an entire suite to herself, and a good meal, a warm bath and a comfortable bed had put her to sleep within minutes of her head touching the pillow. She had got her crying over with in the bath.

Her luggage from the bed-and-breakfast place where she had been staying in Reading was waiting for her when she wakened. Dressed in casual chino pants with a stretchy waist-band and a green T-shirt, she had just finished eating her breakfast when someone knocked on the door. Assuming it was Room Service, coming back to clear the table, Maddie opened the door without making use of the spyhole.

'I see you know who I am. May I come in?' Krista Spyridou asked.

Maddie went white, and then red with discomfiture. It was Krista who closed the door and strolled gracefully across to a chair to make herself at home. Maddie could not take her eyes off the other woman. With her fabulous platinum blonde hair falling round her narrow shoulders like a silk curtain, and her turquoise eyes slashing a bright slice of colour in her flawless face, Krista's glowing perfection took Maddie's breath away.

'I can see you're embarrassed,' Krista remarked with enviable poise. 'But there's really no need to be. I have the solution to all our problems.'

Aghast at the descent of a woman whom she knew she had wounded, Maddie hovered in the centre of the carpet. 'I don't know what to say to you. You must hate me.'

'Why? If it hadn't been you in his bed it would have been some other woman. Giannis lives by his own rules, and I wouldn't dream of interfering. I feel privileged to be a part of his life. He's a very special man,' Krista murmured with a cool smile. 'But this pregnancy of yours does create a problem.'

'How did you even know I was pregnant?' With Krista talking as though her relationship with Giannis was ongoing, Maddie's unease was increasing at a rapid pace.

'Haven't you seen the pictures in the newspapers yet? They were taken yesterday, outside the clinic. Not very flattering of you, I'm afraid. But you're definitely pregnant.' Krista released a musical laugh. 'Anything relating to Giannis Petrakos is always very big news.'

Maddie tried to hide her chagrin. 'I'm sorry, but I don't want to talk about my private life with you.'

'If you care about the future of your twins, you will listen to what I have to say.'

Maddie went very still. 'How did you know I'm having twins?'

Krista looked calmly back at her. 'How do you think? Giannis told me…'

Maddie's skin went clammy and she turned away, speared by that declaration like a fish on a hook. She felt quite sick at the idea of Giannis discussing her predicament with this woman. She also felt rather scared of this beautiful blonde in her ice-blue designer suit, with diamonds twinkling in her earlobes and at her slender throat.

'Let's concentrate on why I'm here,' Krista continued. 'I have a proposition to put to you.'

'I don't want to be rude…but what's any of this got to do with you?' Maddie was struggling desperately to retain some semblance of dignity. 'I understood that you were no longer engaged to Giannis.'

'Giannis and I are very close friends. We've broken up before, but he always comes back to me. This is a messy situation, and I'm happy to help Giannis to sort it out.'

Maddie's hands coiled into defensive fists. She felt gutted and utterly humiliated. 'Then go and talk to him about it.'

'No, this is between us. I'm willing to adopt your children when they're born.'

Maddie was dumbfounded by that assurance, and she spun round wide-eyed. 'You can't be serious!'

'It would be the best solution for everyone. Giannis and I will get married, as we've always planned, and bring the children up together. It's perfect.'

Repulsed by the very suggestion, Maddie stared at the smiling blonde and wondered if it was true that Giannis would go back to her. Krista was so very confident that it was hard to believe what she said did not have a solid basis in fact. 'Does Giannis know you're here?'

Krista elevated a pencilled brow. 'What do you think?'

Maddie's heart sank, and a creepy chill ran down her taut spine. Was this her reward for defying Giannis's wishes and insisting on her independence? Certainly Giannis had to be very close to Krista if he had already shared so much about Maddie with her, his ex-fiancée. Maddie felt as gutted as if Krista had taken a fish-knife to her.

'Obviously Giannis feels responsible for your children.'

'He doesn't have to. I'll manage fine on my own,' Maddie hastened to declare.

'But Giannis will not tolerate that,' the blonde protested. 'He's a Petrakos, and he's used to total control. Don't you understand what that means? If he's not satisfied that you are a perfect parent, he'll take your children away from you.'

Maddie flinched.

'You really haven't a clue.' Krista Spyridou gave an impatient shake of her head. 'Giannis is very powerful and very ruthless when it comes to getting what he wants. If I adopt your children he'll be delighted, and he'll ensure that you never have to work or worry about money again.'

'I have no intention of giving my children up!' Maddie told the blonde in angry disgust. 'And no amount of money will change my mind on that score.'

'I would treat them as my own.' Krista kept on talking in the same relentlessly upbeat tone, flatly refusing to recognise Maddie's revulsion. 'I'm trying to help you—help *all* of us. If you don't watch out you'll lose your children anyway. Giannis wants them. Wouldn't they be better off being raised by their father within marriage? What have you got to offer them?'

Maddie yanked open the door. 'Please leave. I'm not interested in discussing this any further.'

Krista settled a card down on the table. 'My phone number. Be sensible and do the right thing. Some day your children will thank you for it.'

It took quite a few minutes for Maddie to calm down after Krista's departure. She felt threatened and intimidated, but more than anything she felt scared—bone-deep scared.

Had Giannis sent Krista as a messenger? Evidently Krista would do anything to please Giannis and get him to the altar—even accept another woman's kids and raise them. Were they conspiring against her? Was the rift between Giannis and the Greek heiress already healed? Had her pregnancy ironically brought them back together?

Her head pounding with tension, Maddie crammed the clothing she had unpacked back into her case. She was leaving without even knowing where she was going. But what choice did she have? She wasn't running away, she reasoned frantically. She was just trying to look out for the future and protect herself. She believed that her unborn babies needed her love, and that nothing would compensate them for the loss of it or her. The very idea of Krista taking her children made her feel ill. The woman had reminded her of a smiling piranha fish. Not an atom of human emotion had the blonde

betrayed during a dialogue that would have taxed mos
women's control to the utmost.

Chilled by that memory, Maddie went down in the lift an
out on to the street.

Giannis was in the middle of a board meeting when he go
the call from Nemos.

'You make sure they don't lose her…not for so much a
ten seconds!' Giannis warned in raw, wrathful Greek. 'Yo
make sure that nothing happens to her as well.'

His lean, powerful face forbidding, he sprang upright, like
lion going in for the kill, and walked out of the conference room
without a word. Maddie was bolting again. He couldn't believe
it. He was furious, affronted, and badly shaken by that news.

What was the matter with her? What was he supposed t
do? Imprison her? Clearly giving her space and allowing he
to go to a hotel had been a serious error of judgement. Actin
like Mr Sensitive had been a tactical disaster. So now it woul
be gloves off, and he would make her understand her limits
In a rage like nothing he had ever experienced, Giannis swung
into his limo.

CHAPTER EIGHT

MADDIE was hurrying breathlessly down the street, hauling her case, when Giannis appeared in front of her. She stopped dead with a gasp, because it seemed to her that he had come out of nowhere.

'Please get into the car. I don't want to see a picture of us staging a public dispute in tomorrow's newspapers,' Giannis breathed with stinging scorn.

His dark golden eyes were blazing. Shock had overpowered Maddie's flight instincts and settled her into stillness. 'I—'

'Those babies are my flesh and blood too,' Giannis cut in fiercely.

Bothered by that reminder more than she wanted to acknowledge, Maddie released her numbed grip on her case and climbed into the limo by the kerb. What else could she do? She stole a wary glance at him, aware that he was in a towering rage. He had prevented her from leaving again. But how had he known what she was planning to do?

'How did you find out?'

'You have your own security team now.'

'You mean you're having me watched?'

'After today's little demonstration, don't expect an apology on that score.' Giannis dealt her a fulminating appraisal. 'If you'd got away sight unseen, I might never have found you again. Is that what I deserve? Have I been so bad to you that I have no right to know that you are safe? No right even to know my own children?'

A combination of shame, frustration and confusion held Maddie stiff in her seat. 'You shouldn't have sent Krista to see me. That experience would've spooked a saint.'

'Krista?' His sleek ebony brows pleated, and his brilliant eyes were suddenly keen as lasers on her strained face. 'You have actually met Krista?'

Maddie jerked her chin in confirmation.

And that was that. Lean, strong profile set like granite, Giannis swept up the phone, punched out a number, and started speaking in Greek, fast and furious. While he conducted the conversation Maddie breathed in and out several times, in an effort to get her composure back. A couple of minutes later he replaced the phone.

'I didn't send Krista to visit you.'

Maddie was reluctant to believe him. Shaken up as she was, she was afraid to trust him. Was he friend or foe? She no longer knew how to tell the difference. She wanted to believe him. Of course she did. But what if he was playing a double game? It would be foolish to ignore the reality that he had to have his own agenda. Was it feasible that Krista Spyridou had been telling her the truth?

'We'll talk at the apartment,' Giannis decreed, stifling his impatience to know what Krista had said during her visit. That was not a possibility he had foreseen, and he felt culpable. The idea that an external event might have spurred Maddie's second flight mollified him a little, but he was heartily tired of being treated like the enemy.

A lift ferried them in silence up to his penthouse apartment, which was all gleaming stone and wood surfaces, with soaring ceilings that put her in mind of a public building. The reception room struck her as no more inviting. Large as a sports pitch, it was sprinkled at intervals with oddly indistinguishable items of furniture and several large pieces of contemporary sculpture.

Maddie wasted no time in getting to the heart of the atmosphere between them. 'Krista approached me with a proposition. Do you know what it was?'

She focused on Giannis, absorbing the sleek, dark vibrance of him in a navy pinstripe business suit. It took great effort to retain her full concentration. *He's the enemy, he's the enemy,* her common sense rhymed, while the rest of her just rejoiced in his lithe, muscular male beauty, his amazing eyes and his liquid grace of movement.

'How would I know?' Giannis shifted a glass lounging chair a few inches in her direction, because she had sat down on the bi-level coffee table.

'Because you must have talked to her last night,' Maddie dared, wondering why he was shifting his works of art around. 'She already knew I was expecting twins.'

'When the press captured photos of us together, I knew I owed Krista a warning call.' His response was level and unapologetic. 'It's one thing to end an engagement, something else to show up in public with a pregnant woman soon afterwards.'

Maddie flushed, her discomfiture pronounced at that reminder of his former ties with Krista. 'Obviously you're still very close to her.'

'I've known her all my life. Look, what is all this about? Why did Krista want to see you?'

Maddie studied him, fighting to hide her suspicions.

'No, I *don't* know why!' With that response Giannis startled and dismayed her. The apparent fact was that he could read her face like an open book, even when she was striving her hardest to be cunning.

'Krista asked me to agree to you and her adopting the twins.'

Giannis grimaced. 'I don't believe you.'

Her teeth gritted at that unexpected comeback. 'Well, she did. She said you and she had broken up and reconciled before, and that adoption would be the perfect solution. She believed that you'd marry her and raise my children with her.'

Giannis raked long brown fingers through his luxuriant black hair. 'Sometimes the female mind amazes me. That was a very resourceful idea for Krista—even if it was mad.'

Listening to him, Maddie was on hyper-alert. Her need to have her worst fears set to rest was not satisfied by that infuriatingly uninformative response. She had hoped he would tell her that it was nonsense that he and Krista had reconciled before—because the existence of such a history made her feel deeply uneasy. She had hoped he would utterly dismiss the idea that he might still end up marrying Krista. When he did neither, Maddie could no longer suppress her fierce apprehension.

She flew to her feet and snapped, 'So you're saying you had nothing whatsoever to do with that scheme of hers?'

Giannis gave her a long, steady appraisal. 'Do I look that crazy? I know you well enough to be aware that you wouldn't even consider such an arrangement.'

'How am I supposed to trust you?'

One little lie of omission, Giannis reflected in raging frustration, and he was still paying for it in spades. Her lack of faith in him was deeply offensive to his sense of honour. He studied her, now seated on his coffee table, Titian hair fanning round her vivid face. In her bright green T-shirt she should have looked remarkably like a leprechaun. Instead there was something extraordinarily sexy about the *au naturel* look she favoured. Her tousled copper curls framed her provocative green eyes and her ripe pink mouth, and the T-shirt was stretched to capacity over the highly feminine abundance of her full breasts. Angry as he was, that view sent an instant shaft of lust to his groin and his even white teeth clenched.

Maddie could feel his gaze on her bosom, and before she even knew what she was doing she had arched her back like a shameless temptress, so that part of her body was more than ever noticeable. She was shocked at the speed with which that wanton prompting came over her, and even more taken aback by the wild pleasure and satisfaction she experienced when he looked at her in that sexual way. He was turning her into a natural-born trollop, she thought, hating herself like poison for her weakness.

She leapt upright and stalked over to the window. Krista had been so cool, so very classy. 'Giannis…'

'We could just get rid of all this aggro in bed, *pedhi mou*,' Giannis murmured thickly.

She folded her arms fast over her bust, terrified her prominent nipples might be showing through her cotton top. He was absolutely without shame. He had no inhibitions whatsoever. What shook her was how much she liked that earthy sexuality of his.

'Maddie…' he murmured silkily, slowly turning her round into the shelter of his lean, powerful body. 'We need each other.'

He curved his hands to the swell of her behind and drew her up against him, making her madly aware of his masculine arousal. There was a slow burn of warmth and moisture flowering between her thighs, and a dulled ache of physical awareness that left her quivering.

It literally hurt her to yank herself back from the very edge of temptation. 'I can't do this...I can't. It's wrong—'

Hot golden eyes smouldering with urgent desire, Giannis gave her a pained appraisal and surrendered himself to the prospect of the only answer he saw to their plight. 'How is it wrong when we're going to get married?'

'We're going to w-what?' she stammered, staring at him.

'What else can we do? It's the only rational option.' His dark features taut, Giannis shrugged a broad shoulder. 'That's why you can trust me. That's why I was furious that you could even consider running away from me again.'

Maddie was trembling with surprise and uncertainty, hanging on his every word, yet still unable to credit that he could be serious. 'I ran away because I felt that I was being threatened. I haven't got the power or the money it would take to fight you if you decided that you wanted to take my children from me.'

'*Theos mou*...why would I do that? Does that make sense to you?' Giannis demanded in exasperation. 'I want my children to grow up with two parents in a secure environment.'

Maddie worried at her lower lip with her teeth. 'But it isn't necessary for us to get married.'

'It is. Who but me will teach them how to be Greek? How to cope with my Petrakos relations? How to handle wealth and privilege? You couldn't meet that challenge without living in my world.'

All of a sudden Maddie understood why Krista had approached her. The beautiful blonde knew Giannis well enough to guess that he would offer marriage to the mother of his unborn children, and she had tried to pre-empt that possibility.

'I don't know what to say…' she whispered, because her thoughts were buzzing like frantic bees inside her head.

'You say yes…and you say it in Greek.' Giannis surveyed her with that sudden flashing charismatic smile of his that made her heart seesaw on its sadly unreliable supports. '*Ne* is the word you need.'

'But you can't want to marry me,' Maddie protested tautly.

'Why not? You have a proven fertility record, and you're amazing in bed, *glika mou*,' Giannis pointed out without hesitation. 'What more is there?'

All the stuff that he wasn't about to offer or deliver, Maddie affixed in angry confusion: love, fidelity, communication. *A proven fertility record?* She wanted to slap him. Why was it that the instant matters took a serious turn Giannis resorted to being facetious? Such a superficial relationship would never be enough for her. But if she didn't marry him he might end up marrying Krista, who was obviously still in hot pursuit. The very thought of Giannis getting hitched to Krista instead sent an icy wave of fear travelling through Maddie—because she knew now that Krista would plot and plan against her and her children. She would be damned if she did agree to marry him, damned if she did not. In neither option did she see the prospect of happiness.

The tip of Maddie's tongue snaked out to moisten her dry lower lip. 'And if I say no?' she prompted.

An explosive silence pooled between them like an oil spill.

Giannis was still, but she could feel the storm within him like a dangerously destructive riptide below the surface. Lush black lashes screened his dark golden eyes and their shimmering glitter of warning. 'Let's not go there,' he drawled, without any inflection at all.

Maddie registered that she did not have a choice. Or at least he had just heavily weighted the marrying option. It was total overkill. She wondered if she should tell him that his threat was quite unnecessary, since she had been brought to her knees just by the idea of Krista walking down the aisle with him. She had a mean, jealous streak a mile wide. She was horribly ashamed of herself. She felt that if she was actually the kind, decent woman she had once believed she was, she would have wanted Giannis to return to Krista. But she loved Giannis, and she knew that she had to do the best she could for her unborn children. His attitude might outrage her, but she would find stronger ground on which to fight back and mount a defence. If he was prepared to coerce her into marriage, Maddie reasoned hotly, he would have to accept the certain consequences of that decision.

Giannis decided that he had probably picked the only woman in the world who would sit pregnant with his twins on his coffee table and quietly spend ten minutes deciding whether or not she would become a Petrakos. While he was not proud of the veiled threat he had employed, he was convinced that the ultimate good of his intentions excused his ruthless methods in obtaining the desired result.

'All right. I'll marry you,' Maddie informed him flatly.

'Do you think you could risk one glass of champagne to celebrate?' An immediate smile of approval slashed his wide sensual mouth.

Her green eyes gleamed. 'I'm not celebrating.'

Giannis did not bat a magnificent eyelash at that declaration. Having achieved his goal, he was in excellent form. Her days of vanishing were at an end. Never again would she go anywhere he couldn't find her. He found that a hugely soothing prospect. During the weeks she had been missing he had been unnerved by the discovery that not even his bottomless resources could help to locate her when there was not a single lead to go on. Her disappearance had been a continual source of disquiet to him, a reality that she did not seem to appreciate.

'I'd like the ceremony to take place as soon as possible.' Giannis rested assessing gilded bronze eyes on her, not entirely certain that he could fully trust her agreement.

'Whatever…' Maddie lifted and dropped a shoulder with an indifference that set his teeth on edge.

'A proper wedding,' Giannis added loftily, just in case he had given her the impression that he was suggesting some shabby affair. 'Church, wedding gown, hundreds of guests.'

Maddie bridled. 'I'm not stuffing myself into a wedding dress when I'm *this* pregnant!'

'*So?*' Giannis challenged. 'You might as well flaunt it. It is not so unusual these days.'

Maddie could think of nothing more guaranteed to embarrass her to death than a pregnant stomach at her wedding, where every one of his friends and relatives would be comparing her to her reed-slender predecessor Krista. While at the same time doubtless blaming her for getting involved with a man already engaged to someone else.

Although the enthusiasm Giannis had hoped to ignite had so far failed to appear, he was nothing if not persistent. Perhaps, he reasoned, she was afraid that she would not be up to the monumental task of organising such an event with only weeks to spare. 'Naturally a wedding planner and my staff will deal with all the arrangements.'

'If I *have* a vote to cast, I go for a quiet hole-and-corner marriage ceremony.'

Keeping a tense grip on his growing vexation, Giannis breathed in slow and deep, before saying with admirable cool, 'I will be proud to make you my wife. A hole-and-corner ceremony is not what I want.'

Maddie looped several bright copper spirals of hair off her brow, and her green eyes glinted like a cat about to claw. 'And of course we all know that what you want you must have. But I'm warning you that if you marry me life isn't going to be as neat and tidy as that.'

'Is that a declaration of war, *pedhi mou*?' Giannis was hugely amused by that idea. He marvelled at the fact that he found her constantly entertaining. Right now she was annoyed with him, but she would get over that and appreciate that he really did know best. Didn't she realise that a small secret wedding would only make it look as if he was ashamed of her and feed the gossips? Didn't all women go mad for weddings? He was convinced that, whatever she said, in no time she would be deeply involved in the preparations. All she required was a little push in the right direction.

'I've got nothing more to say on that score. But where am I supposed to live in the meantime?'

'Here.'

Maddie grimaced.

Giannis rose to the bait. 'It's a fabulous apartment.'

Maddie sniffed. 'It's a bit James Bond, though, isn't it? You don't even own a comfortable seat.'

Giannis rose above the desire to tell her that she might have had a different opinion had she not been seated on a coffee table. 'If you don't like this place it's not a problem. I have a country house in Kent.'

'If you don't mind, I'll stay there until the wedding.' Out of easy reach of him and all temptation, Maddie thought ruefully.

Giannis did mind—very much. He said nothing, though. He understood that he had used coercion, and she was hitting out with the only weapons at her disposal. He was disconcerted by the speed with which she had learned how to fight back. Had she learned that art from him? He wondered how fast a wedding could be organised. Two weeks? A month? He didn't want to wait a month. If he was honest with himself, he didn't want to wait a week. He was astonished at the driving force of his impatience. He was, after all, the same guy who had insisted Krista pick a wedding date more than eighteen months ahead.

Ten days later, there was an expectant hush in the elegant drawing-room of Harriston Hall once the lawyer had finished explaining the salient points of the pre-nuptial agreement to Maddie.

She had been shaken when she heard that, in the event of a marital breakdown, Giannis expected to retain custody of their children. It seemed to her that the inclusion of such a condition implied that he was betting on their marriage failing, and was unlikely to make the effort to ensure that their relationship survived.

'Giannis retains custody regardless of who is at fault?' Maddie queried. 'That's totally unfair.'

'I'm afraid fault doesn't come into it.'

'Well, it should,' Maddie told the lawyer roundly. 'I presume I can make conditions too?'

'Of course. But it will extend these negotiations,' the suave older man warned her, as if he expected that fact to put her off.

Maddie almost smiled. 'That's fine by me. I won't accept that clause concerning the children. My stipulation is that if Giannis breaks his marriage vows he has to surrender his right to retain custody.'

Unprepared for that announcement, the lawyer gave her a startled look, before professionalism smoothed over his face again.

'I do appreciate that Giannis won't like that.' Her eyes gleamed like emeralds, startlingly vivid against her white skin. 'I also think that, since fidelity is very important to me, there should be a clause that discourages him from the pursuit of other women.'

Her companion was now regarding her in total fascination. He had been planning how he would describe the future Mrs Petrakos to his interested colleagues, for she was a source of enormous curiosity. Exotic, unusual, sexy…but the extraordinary *je-ne-sais-quoi* that had netted her a billionaire bridegroom had eluded his detection. Now he saw that quality in neon lights. The bride might be pregnant, but she was in no hurry to get to the church, and she was voicing her controversial demands with composure. She was exactly the kind of woman who would take a tiger by the tail. Or, in this case, a notorious womaniser.

'What exactly were you thinking of?'

Maddie was considering what was most important to Giannis. His reputation? His power? His wealth? He was incredibly serious about business and the art of making money. Perhaps the knowledge that infidelity would cost him money would act as a deterrent? And, if it did not, at least she would have the satisfaction of being rich in her own right, as well as wretched. 'If he is unfaithful, it should cost him millions.'

'I believe that a clause of that nature would raise quite a storm,' the older man cautioned.

'I'm sure it will.' But Maddie was not prepared to back down. If Giannis was determined to marry her, he would have to make choices too. He could not have everything his way.

'What sort of a financial figure do you have in mind as a disincentive to a straying husband?' he enquired.

'A figure that would hurt.'

The lawyer could hardly wait to lay that tantalising and explosive prospect before the haughty Petrakos legal team, who had made it clear that they expected the pre-nup to be signed immediately and without even a minor quibble. He wondered which fall guy would get the thankless task of briefing Giannis Petrakos on his bride-to-be's punitive take on adultery.

After his departure, Maddie went for a walk in the grounds of the house. Harriston Hall was a very comfortable Edwardian mansion that had been remodelled so extensively inside that very little of the original property remained. It was as sumptuous as a hotel, and its staff could not do enough to make her feel comfortable. After several nights of undisturbed sleep and regular meals, her bone-deep tiredness and almost all the sickness had gradually faded away. She was feeling healthier and stronger. Since she had left London she had seen Giannis only once, and that had been in the first few days when he had flown in for lunch *en route* for Brussels. Her coolness had washed off him like ice-cream left out in the sun. He had nerves of steel. But she was pretty certain that the clause she wanted inserted in the pre-nup would bring Giannis down to visit again. She was looking forward to that prospect…

That evening, Maddie was enjoying a long, lazy soak in her *en-suite* bathroom when a sharp knock sounded on the door. She sat up with a start, water sloshing noisily around her. 'Yes?' she called out.

'It's Giannis…' The door swung open.

Maddie let out a muffled shriek and crossed her arms over her rounded tummy. 'Don't you dare come in!'

'Don't keep me waiting,' Giannis intoned. 'Can you manage on your own? Or would you like me to play lady's maid?'

'I'm not the size of a house yet!' Maddie exclaimed, standing up, water streaming off her in rivulets as she snatched frantically at a towel. She got a glimpse of herself in the mirror and very nearly groaned out loud. She was pink all over, like a freshly boiled lobster, and her mass of curls was anchored to the top of her head by a lime-green clip in the shape of a dog.

From the other side of the bedroom Giannis studied her as she emerged, swathed from neck to toe in a very large towel. The silence literally screamed.

'If you give me five minutes, I'll get dressed,' she told him in a rush.

'In those rags?' Giannis scooped up the shortie pyjamas lying on the bed, and tossed them down again in contemptuous dismissal. The sight of that familiar set acted as an inflammatory reminder of Morocco, where matters had swung from paradise to hell and out of his control. 'You reject everything I give you…you reject who I am!'

Maddie gulped. 'I—'

'What interest have you even taken in your own wedding?' His complete incomprehension on that score was as palpable as the truth that he had been deeply offended by her display of uninterest. 'If you ruin it, you can't have it over again!'

Maddie found herself squirming. The flash of masculine bewilderment she recognised in his penetrating gaze made her feel bad. Her sole intent had been to demonstrate to him that she wasn't prepared to act the joyful bride when she had given her consent under duress. But hadn't she already decided that she would marry him anyway? Was it his fault he hadn't appreciated that she had no intention of letting him go free? And was she prepared to let her pride spoil her wedding day?

'But what I cannot excuse is that you should choose to denounce my standards of behaviour through my own lawyers!' Giannis raked at her in condemnation. 'How could you do that?'

CHAPTER NINE

His strong face clenched, Giannis was even angrier than Maddie had anticipated.

'I thought it was okay to say anything I liked to a solicitor hired to represent my interests.'

'What gave you that idea?' Giannis challenged, without skipping a beat 'The word "anything" covers a lot of ground that I would not have taken into the public arena!'

'Well, you didn't have a problem with me being told that if our marriàge broke up you would get to keep the children,' Maddie reminded him. 'How much more personal can you get?'

Giannis stilled for a moment in his restive passage round the spacious room and shot her a dark-as-midnight glance that revealed nothing. 'That is not the point.'

'It's exactly the point,' she declared. 'That was a major part of the pre-nuptial agreement. Yet you didn't see any need to discuss those terms with me in private beforehand. Of course *you* don't discuss anything.'

Even though he was well aware of his evasive tactics in that department, Giannis growled, 'What's that supposed to mean?'

'How dare you let your lawyers sit and talk over how I'm

going to lose my children when you're the one most likely to wreck the marriage in the first place!'

At that ringing indictment of his character, dulled coins of colour accentuated the superb line of his classic Petrakos cheekbones. 'I don't accept that.'

'Marriage is something that I take very seriously.' Maddie lifted her chin.

His dark eyes had the icy glitter of stars, and she knew his temper was under wraps again. 'As do I…hence the pre-nup. But I take very strong exception to the demands that you saw fit to voice through your lawyer!'

'You didn't give me much of a choice about marrying you, but at least I have more sense than to go plunging into it without foreseeing the pitfalls and trying to avoid them!' Maddie launched back at him with conviction.

'But all you ever see is pitfalls and problems! What happened to trust and optimism? I believe that I will be an exceptional husband.' Giannis slung that assurance back at her without hesitation, for he had spent every free moment during the past ten days trying to decide on the wedding details that she had yet to show the smallest interest in. 'But face it now…I will *not* stoop to sign an agreement which tries to tell me what I can and cannot do in my life!'

'Has anyone *ever* tried to impose boundaries on you?' Maddie was genuinely curious on that score, because it seemed to her that Giannis had always done exactly as he liked while utterly refusing to acknowledge his mistakes.

His stubborn jaw line squared. 'I have complete faith in my ability to choose my own boundaries,' he spelt out grittily.

'Do you think that attitude might possibly explain why you're now on the brink of a shotgun marriage?' Maddie dared, fighting back with all her might. 'Engaged to one woman, sleeping with another? It was a recipe for disaster.'

Pure outrage at that unbelievably tactless reminder assailed Giannis. His golden eyes smouldered like the heart of a fire, his ferocious pride stung. 'I will not discuss this with you any more,' he framed thickly, striding towards the door. 'I cannot—'

'Yes, you can,' Maddie protested, dismayed that he was planning to walk out on her.

'You are a pregnant woman and you shouldn't be getting upset. I can't argue with you like this!'

Pregnant or not, Maddie made it to the door ahead of him. She plastered her back to it and spread her arms as if she was ready to barricade him in and hold him prisoner if necessary. 'Don't be daft…of course you can argue with me! I'm tough. I can take it. What do you think I'm made of? Glass?'

'Glorious curves.' His masculine attention was unashamedly locked to her voluptuous shape. As she'd raced across the room her towel had slid down several inches, and the luscious swell of her creamy breasts was now shockingly prominent over its fleecy edge.

Maddie met his stunning eyes and a wicked little coil of heat spread wanton fingers of awareness through all the tender, responsive parts of her body. Knowing that if she stayed there one second longer Giannis would be more than willing to employ sex as a distraction, she stepped away from the door and put some sensible space between them.

'We don't have to argue…we just need to talk,' Maddie reasoned soothingly.

Giannis didn't want to talk. He just wanted to take her towel off and sink himself into her delicious pink and white body until the tumult of his irate thoughts stilled and the tormenting ache of lust was quenched.

'Please don't go,' Maddie urged, desperate to keep him with her. 'I really do want our marriage to work.'

A tiny amount of his sceptical tension ebbed, and he swung back to face her again.

'You see…it's not a matter of anyone trying to tell you what to do. You picked that up all wrong,' she assured him winningly. 'I know that wouldn't work.'

Giannis felt reassured enough to let his rigid shoulders rest back against the solid wood door.

'I mean, the way I see it the choice is all yours. We can have a marriage that's just a façade—'

A slight frown began to divide his sleek ebony brows again. 'A façade?'

'For the sake of the children. We'd share everything to do with them and you could do as you liked with other women.'

Giannis tensed. He didn't know what she was about to say next. Knowing her views, he was extremely suspicious of such uncritical candour. She had also managed to make that option sound sleazy rather than liberated. 'What are you getting at?'

'Well, it would be sort of marriage-*lite*, as I see it. We'd pretty much lead separate lives.'

'Separate?' Giannis was getting disturbing vibes about the offer of marriage-*lite*, as she called it. It sounded like a poisoned chalice.

Maddie flushed. 'Well, obviously we wouldn't be sharing a bedroom—'

Giannis shook his arrogant dark head in instantaneous rejection. 'Sounds more like marriage-*hell* than marriage-*lite*. Don't ever take a job as a saleswoman.'

'But if you can't commit to fidelity that sort of marriage will suit you best.'

Giannis stretched back against the door like a hungry predator, wakening to find a three-course lunch parading past. His brilliant eyes gleamed.

His silence put Maddie more on edge. 'There would be obvious benefits. At least we'd be accepting each other as we are.'

'Me the eternal sinner and you the suffering saint of restraint?' Giannis quipped with rich cynicism

'No. Eventually we'd forget…well, you know…that we had ever slept together,' she muttered self-consciously. 'And then we'd be able to be friends.'

Giannis shook his handsome head in vehement rejection of that hope, and jerked his thumb down like a Roman emperor ordering the death penalty. 'I take it option two is following my marriage vows or being fined millions and millions for breaking your rules?'

Maddie winced. 'That's a very emotive way of putting it.'

'How would you describe it, *glikia mou*?'

'I just need you to take marrying me seriously,' she admitted.

'Marriage-*heavy*?' Giannis breathed in silken derision. 'If I do as I'm told, you'll condescend to share my bed? Forget it… Greece doesn't breed wimps who let their women call the shots.'

'Where is it written that a Greek tycoon has to have a mistress?' Maddie suddenly launched at him in furious frustration. 'Aren't I enough for you? How would you feel if I got another man?'

All pretence of relaxation banished, Giannis flipped away from the doorframe and strode forward, dark eyes bright with aggression. 'Don't even *think* about it. I wouldn't tolerate even a flirtation. Not for one moment!'

Maddie sent him a winging glance. 'I won't make the obvious comment.'

'*Theos* mou…are you calling me a hypocrite?'

'I don't suppose it much matters—since we probably won't be getting married now anyway. After all, it doesn't look like either of us is going to sign that pre-nup.' There was a tiny catch in Maddie's voice, for it was not the conclusion she had dimly envisaged. Unfortunately she had not thought through to the likely end result of her strategy. Why hadn't it occurred to her that she was dealing with a virile male to whom machismo was a matter of pride and honour? There she had been, thinking she was so smart, but she had boxed herself into a corner with her own options.

In the uneasy silence Giannis expelled his breath on a slow hiss. Darkly handsome features bleak, he surveyed her with level deep-set eyes that had an extraordinary intensity. He wasn't backing down; he never backed down.

Without another word he walked out of the room. He took the stairs two at a time and called for the limo to be brought round. While he waited he poured a brandy. He was so angry he paced the room like a tiger trapped in a cage. When he was told that the car was waiting, he found himself reluctant to take advantage of it. He had come down to stay the night, and he would stay. *She* was the one who ran away from problems. He frowned. Had she had any other choice? He had put too much pressure on her and damaged her ability to trust him. Was it fair to blame her for that? He no longer had a mistress in his life.

Giannis brooded on his ferocious dissatisfaction over a

second brandy, and soon found more suitable culprits to hold responsible. It was the lawyers who had brought them to this unhappy pass! How could Maddie understand an agreement which had primarily been designed to protect his great wealth? She hadn't a greedy bone in her body. She was the only woman he had ever met who ignored his riches and dealt with him as a man. That might often have proved to be an uncomfortable experience, but she was not the potential gold-digger that the pre-nup had been drawn up to frustrate. Nor, he was convinced, would she ever do anything to harm their children.

He wondered if she was aware that the history of marriage in the Petrakos clan was a long and unhappy one. Bitter divorces, court battles for custody and explosive scandal had dogged every generation but one. His great-grandparents had been the last happily married couple in his immediate family. Rodas Petrakos had married his childhood sweetheart, Dorkas, in the teeth of all opposition. There had been no pre-nup and, although by all accounts it had been a volatile marriage, the couple had stayed together. Along the way both parties must have made compromises and trade-offs, but the legal profession had been kept out of it. Perhaps, Giannis decided, it was unwise to allow such private matters to be dealt with by third parties. In fact perhaps all that talk of negative expectations had merely made Maddie feel threatened, insecure and unappreciated.

When a knock sounded on the door, Maddie pulled herself awkwardly up against the pillows. 'Yes?'

Giannis strolled in, shorn of his jacket and tie, his blue designer shirt open at his strong brown throat.

Maddie blinked in surprise, for she had heard the limo

driving round from the garage block and had honestly believed that he was gone. 'You're still here?'

Giannis inclined his arrogant dark head. 'I have an early flight tomorrow. It would make no sense to leave. Even I need to sleep.'

'Oh.' It dawned on her that her eyes had to be pink and swollen, because she had been crying, but mercifully he was not looking directly at her. Indeed he seemed to be extremely interested in the carved post at the foot of the bed. 'Is there something up?'

His proud dark head came up at that enquiry, liquid golden eyes wary beneath the heavy fringe of his spiky lashes. 'No, but I have reached a decision. We will dispense with the prenuptial agreement. It is surplus to requirements.'

She had breathed in deep when he said he had reached a decision, bracing herself as if she was waiting for the roof to fall down and crush her. But when he mentioned dispensing with the agreement she was bemused. She almost parted her lips to ask about the marriage choices she had offered, and then she sealed them shut again. Was he avoiding the issue? Saving face? Or still thinking his options over? Why not get him past the altar and then settle down into reforming him from the ground up? It was a low, sneaky thought, and she was ashamed of herself, but she was fast reaching the conclusion that direct confrontation was unproductive. He was an Alpha male high-achiever, programmed to compete and fight when challenged. She needed to be more subtle. After all, no matter how annoyed she got with him, she loved him to bits and knew all too well how unhappy she would be without him.

'All right…' Maddie agreed, her attention lingering on the blue-black shadow of stubble darkening his strong jawline. He looked drop-dead gorgeous, and her pulses quickened along with her heartbeat. 'You need a shave. You look like a pirate,' she added without thinking.

Relief that he was not being greeted with a barrage of questions brought a smile of amusement to his handsome mouth. 'I do have a yacht.'

'I saw it on television,' she confessed.

A sleek ebony brow elevated in polite surprise. 'How? When?'

Maddie went pink and grimaced. 'After I got back from Morocco I saw a documentary about you and Krista.'

'You watched that tacky programme?' Giannis demanded.

Maddie nodded ruefully.

His tension dropped yet another notch. Now he knew why she saw him as a womaniser. No wonder his marriage proposal had got a cool reception, he reflected, glad to have that ego-zapping truth clarified. 'It was full of nonsensical errors and wild exaggerations about my lifestyle. I was misrepresented.'

'All those supermodels?'

'I've moved on from that stage in my life,' Giannis drawled with supreme cool.

Maddie knew that she could not compare to such women, and she tried hard to avoid that train of thought. She could see little point in bemoaning the reality that she was not taller, thinner, more traffic-stoppingly good-looking. In choosing his companions from the ranks of the most beautiful women available he had only done what other rich young men tended to do. But it was difficult to avoid the reflection that he was only with her because she had conceived his children.

Giannis was noticing the pale purplish shadows below her reddened eyes. Exhaustion and strain were etched in her pallor, and suddenly he was furious with himself, not only for allowing her to get in that condition but also for contributing to her distress. 'It's the early hours of the morning, *pedhi mou*,' he murmured quietly. 'You should be resting.'

'Stay…' Maddie heard herself whisper, without even being aware that she was about to say it.

After an instant of hesitation Giannis lowered himself gracefully down beside her on the bed. Scarcely crediting his presence, she lay so still that she hardly dared to breathe. He snaked an arm round her and eased her back against him.

'Go to sleep,' he urged. 'You look incredibly tired.'

Maddie could have done without that information, as she was already painfully aware that she was not looking her best, but the heat and solidarity of his lean, powerful body next to hers was amazingly soothing. The faint familiar tang of his cologne flared her nostrils and, weary though she was, stark hunger for a greater intimacy stirred delicious tension in her.

Giannis let his hands slide below her camisole top to rest on the place where her waist had once been. 'May I?' he whispered huskily.

'Anything you like,' she muttered, a slight quiver rippling through her as she voiced her gruff invitation.

But it was her pregnant shape that had provoked his interest. His lean hands were very gentle, his long, shapely fingers splaying in slow, uncharacteristically tentative exploration over the gentle swell of her stomach. 'Amazing…' he commented, his breath fanning her cheek.

Giannis felt a little flicker below his palm. When it became more pronounced, he murmured in a tone of awe, 'Is that one of the babies kicking?'

'Yes, they're very active,' Maddie said in a small voice, rec-

ognising that at that moment he was much more entranced
with the miracle of conception than her far-from-perfect body.

Maddie listened to the buzz of a language other than her own
at the far end of the stateroom and smiled.

In every way that mattered, her wedding promised to be
Greek in nature. The day before she had flown out to board
her bridegroom's yacht, *Libos I,* which was cruising the
Aegean Sea. Determined to protect their privacy as far as
possible, Giannis had so far succeeded in ensuring that the
wedding location was unknown to the media. Aware that
Maddie had no family to perform the usual ceremonial roles,
he had also, with her agreement, invited two of his cousins to
act as her bridesmaids. Although Apollina and Desma were
deeply in awe of Giannis, the vivacious brunettes had quickly
lost their cautious manner around Maddie.

Maddie was amused that her attendants were so preoccu-
pied with their private conversation that they had just about
forgotten about her. 'That must be some juicy piece of gossip
the two of you are sharing!'

The sisters broke out of their huddle and sent her tense
glances. 'Gossip?' Apollina queried worriedly.

'I was only teasing you.'

'Only teasing…' Desma repeated with an air of relief.

'Is there something wrong?' Maddie prompted, for it
seemed to her that both young women were rather on edge.

Apollina, the older sister, moved closer. 'Of course there
is nothing wrong. You look wonderful, Maddie.'

'It's a fantastic dress.' Maddie turned and twisted in front
of the tall mirror, endeavouring to see herself from every con-
ceivable angle. The beaded lace bodice and narrow sleeves

were fitted and stylish. Glorious textured silk fell from below the bust and did a remarkable job of skimming over her tummy. Shimmering pearls had been patiently strung through her hair, and she felt truly glamorous for the first time in her life. A magnificent heart-shaped diamond pendant glittered at her throat. A wedding gift from Giannis, it had been delivered to her over breakfast.

'It's not the dress—it is you who looks wonderful,' Desma corrected. 'When they see you, everyone will understand why Giannis fell in love with you.'

Maddie's eyes shadowed. She wandered over to the window and realised that the huge vessel was finally heading towards land, after spending more than twenty-four hours in the open sea. Apollina and Desma were just trying to be kind, she thought ruefully. The sisters probably had no idea that she had barely seen Giannis over the past three weeks. He had slept beside her that one night at Harriston Hall, but he hadn't touched her, and he had been gone by the time she wakened. In fact they had not made love since Morocco. Recently she had seen him only twice, and then in company. He had held her hand with the sort of awkwardness that suggested he didn't really know what to do once he had it, and on three separate occasions he had kissed her brow and her cheek as if she was a little old lady or a child. Evidently her sex appeal had headed in much the same direction as her waist, and what was she supposed to do about that?

'That's Libos.' Apollina had joined her by the window. 'What could be more perfect for a secluded wedding than a private island?'

Having answered the phone, Desma passed the receiver to Maddie.

'What do you think of your future home?' Giannis asked.

A thickly wooded green headland ran all the way down to a white beach lapped by sparkling turquoise blue water. Hills studded by tall cypresses surrounded a picturesque village with white houses and a harbour. 'It's truly beautiful… It sounds trite, but it's just like a postcard—the sort you want to walk right into,' she confided shyly.

'Go out on deck—you'll get the best view from there.'

Impervious to her bridesmaids' lamentations, Maddie went out onto the viewing terrace beyond her stateroom. Her copper curls blew back in the breeze, but she was smiling like mad while Giannis carefully directed her attention to various landmarks and explained that his villa was not visible from the sea.

'Where are you?' she prompted.

'Down at the harbour, having a last drink as a single man. See you in ten minutes, *pedhi mou*.'

The familiar sound of his dark, deep drawl had banished her anxiety about the future. *Libos I* docked, and the crew lined up to wish her well before she walked down the gangway. She was enchanted by the beribboned open carriage and two white horses waiting to collect her. The church had a tall tiered bell-tower, and presided in some state over an elegant square that seemed surprisingly large for a small village.

Giannis strode down the steps to help her from the carriage. In a formal suit, with his black hair gleaming in the sunshine, lean bronzed features unusually expressive as he smiled, he was downright irresistible. In the instant before she stepped out she was madly aware of the close scrutiny of his dark golden appraisal.

'You look incredible.'

'What do you think of the dress?'

Ignoring the step, Giannis lifted her down, his gaze hot with very masculine appreciation. 'Very, very sexy,' he breathed in a roughened undertone.

'But it doesn't show *anything*!' she whispered in dismay.

'I've got a photographic memory,' Giannis husked with lazy amusement as he slowly lowered her to the ground.

Only really conscious of Giannis, Maddie was obediently still while her bridesmaids fussed with the short train on her dress and twitched her mane of hair into place. Suddenly she was wondering what she had been worried about and why she had been so tense. Wasn't she about to marry the guy she loved?

The church was packed with people. There was an audible gasp as they entered. Her bemused attention swept over the colourful frescoes, the masses of flowers and the sombre priest. The rich scent of incense discernible in the still air, the ceremony began. The solemn ritual engaged Maddie from the outset, and when the guests showered the newly married pair with flower petals her heart felt full to overflowing.

Afterwards, the carriage swept them through the village and up a winding wooded road that climbed into the hills. The Petrakos villa was much older than she had expected. Giannis explained that his family's ties with Libos stretched back more than a century. His acquisition of the island had been much more recent, and designed to protect it from excessive development. Surrounded by superb grounds that ran right down to the beach, the magnificent villa enjoyed glorious views of the sea. Giannis carried his bride over the threshold in true English style, and Maddie was laughing when the first guests arrived.

With Giannis by her side for support, she began to meet his relatives and friends. Names and faces swiftly blurred. The sheer number of guests was overwhelming. Many spoke English, but she resolved to learn some basic Greek as soon as she could. During the lengthy meal she tried not to appear conscious that she was the cynosure of all eyes.

'Why are so many people staring at me?' she finally asked Apollonia.

After several glasses of champagne, the youthful brunette was very giggly. 'How many reasons do you want? Today you became a very influential woman, because you're the wife of a very powerful and rich man. You also snatched Giannis from Krista at the eleventh hour. The family is hugely curious about you, and probably wondering how much of what they read in the newspaper about you is true!'

'What newspaper?' Maddie pressed in bewilderment.

Apollonia clapped a hand to her mouth, aghast. 'Giannis said you weren't to be told. Please don't tell him it was me!'

And with that plea her bridesmaid fled.

Giannis took Maddie on to the dance floor. She tried to hold her curiosity in, and couldn't. 'What was in what newspaper about me?' she asked finally. 'Was it a British one?'

Giannis stiffened with distaste. 'Yes. My lawyers are on it—'

'But what did it say?'

'Nothing of any consequence.'

'I insist—'

'Insisting won't get you anywhere, *pedhi mou*,' Giannis told her squarely. 'You're a Petrakos now. The press are beneath your notice.'

'Don't talk to me as if I'm a child,' Maddie argued, only half beneath her breath.

His hard jawline clenched. 'Then behave like an adult.

This is our wedding, and you're making it obvious that we're having a disagreement.'

'I dare say Krista would've behaved much better,' Maddie snapped back.

'Her behaviour in public is always impeccable,' Giannis said drily.

Maddie, who had already been feeling bad for making a snide comment, was further punished by the swiftness with which he confirmed her worst expectations. She was a jealous cat, she thought painfully, and he was ashamed of her.

The remainder of the dance took place in silence, with Maddie wearing a small fixed smile, her wide eyes prickling as she studied the lapel of his jacket. She left the floor then, keen to find a private corner, and was within a few feet of leaving the vast ballroom when a walking stick fell in front of her.

Picking it up, Maddie passed it back to the tiny old lady seated in the alcove on her own. 'Here you are…'

A thin, frail hand caught hers. 'Come and sit by me. I'm your husband's great-grandmother—Dorkas.'

After the briefest of hesitations, Maddie sat down

'Giannis has always reminded me of my late husband Rodas,' Dorkas confessed. 'He's obstinate, impatient, and too clever for his own good.'

Maddie gave her a disconcerted look, registering that those shrewd dark eyes must have spotted the tension between bride and groom. She went pink. 'Yes.'

'But while Rodas had the good luck to be born into a loving family, Giannis was less fortunate.' Dorkas compressed her creased lips. 'How much do you know about your husband's background?'

'He doesn't like to talk about it.'

The old lady sighed. 'His parents should never have had children. Every day was a party for them. Giannis was raised by servants. His mother became a drug addict, but it was covered up. Nobody wanted a scandal. Giannis never knew love or stability, or even kindness from them…'

Maddie was shaken by the bleak picture the old lady was painting. 'I had no idea.'

'When he was sixteen, the only person who had ever loved him in that household died, and he went a little crazy for a while. Happily, he found himself again. He is very strong,' Dorkas Petrakos asserted with proud affection. 'But he needs an equally strong wife who knows how to smooth away the rough edges and love him.'

Maddie was already recapturing her usual calm.

'Rodas and I had many battles, but when anyone dared to say a word against me he was a lion in my defence,' the old lady confided.

Maddie grinned. 'You've heard about that newspaper story, haven't you?'

The beady black eyes gleamed with ready humour. 'I have a copy in my handbag.'

'Could I see it?'

Dorkas passed a folded sheet of paper to her. It was a photocopy which she confided had been faxed from London by an old friend.

Maddie winced at the headline: *Office temp steals Petrakos from heiress.*

'Giannis didn't take such stealing, did he?' Dorkas chuckled. 'He wasn't happy with Krista. As for the rest of it— hold your head up high. Love is not a sin, and children are a blessing to a warm heart. You're a fine young woman—hard-working, and you were caring towards your elderly relatives. Few people here today could say as much.'

His astute dark eyes trained on Maddie and Dorkas, Giannis approached, amusement curving his expressive mouth. 'What do you think of her?' he asked his great-grandmother boldly.

A satisfied smile on her creased face, Dorkas patted Maddie's knee. 'This one is a treasure. Look after her.'

Giannis sat down to chat to the old lady for a while, and then the famous singer he'd had flown in for the reception put on a fabulous performance for them.

Night was falling when Giannis walked Maddie out on to a private terrace, screened from the more public areas by lush green vegetation. Gilded bronze eyes scanning her upturned face in possessive appraisal, he claimed a slow, sensual kiss that sent a shiver of reaction travelling down her slender spine.

'There's a staircase behind the door in the corner. Our suite is at the top of it. I'll join you there in five minutes,' he asserted.

'But we can't just vanish—'

'Yes, we can,' he told her, tasting her ripe pink mouth with even greater fervour. 'This is our wedding night, *agape mou*.'

The huge, beautifully furnished bedroom was dimly lit and intimate. She was just breathing in the glorious scent of an arrangement of roses in a silver bowl when a knock sounded on the door. A maid passed her a phone with what sounded like an apology.

'Hello…who am I speaking to?' Maddie was frowning, feeling sure the call was not for her and that in two seconds flat someone would start chattering in Greek.

'It's Krista.'

Maddie's skin turned clammy, her fingers tightening round the receiver in dismay. 'Why are you calling me?'

'It's your wedding night, and I want you to appreciate that all we've done is swap roles,' Krista murmured sweetly. 'You were the mistress and now I am. Giannis has no intention of giving me up. Did you think he would? All that matters to him right now is keeping you happy because you're expecting those precious twins. But I'm as much a part of his life as I've always been.'

On that poisonous note, the phone went dead. Maddie set it down with a clumsy hand. What a vindictive woman! Of course what Krista had said wasn't true. It was just horrible nasty lies, designed to worry and wound. Krista wanted to upset her and cause trouble.

Maddie told herself that she was too sensible to pay heed to such claims. Her wedding day had been wonderful. She loved Giannis and she had to have faith in him. To doubt him on the word of an angry, spiteful woman would be to destroy what they did have.

CHAPTER TEN

GIANNIS strolled through the door and watched Maddie shimmy her curvaceous hips, sending her wedding gown down over them into a frothy wave of lace and silk round her ankles. She stood revealed in a low-cut bra, minuscule panties and lace hold-up stockings. A blue garter encircled one slender thigh as a finishing touch. He was enthralled.

'Hold it there, *pedhi mou*,' Giannis urged. 'Let me take care of the rest.'

Maddie blushed, for she hadn't heard him come in. It was so long since they had shared a bed that she felt wildly self-conscious. A charismatic smile on his lips, he shed his jacket and tie and unbuttoned his dress shirt. The entire time he watched her like a hawk. 'Do you know?' he murmured conversationally. 'I've never gone so long without sex in my life.'

Taken aback by that admission, Maddie gave him a startled look, and then she started to giggle, all her tension dissolving.

Giannis scored long brown fingers through his luxuriant black hair. 'I didn't intend to say said that—'

'Oh, I'm so glad that you did. I thought you didn't want me any more,' Maddie whispered, closing the space between them and stretching up on tiptoe to share that fear. She wondered how long it had been since he was with another woman. Just as quickly she squashed that thought. Because she was convinced that since the day he learned that she was pregnant, he had been true to her.

Giannis gave her an amused look and slowly shook his handsome dark head. 'Where did you get that idea? Initially I thought restraint was a necessity. You looked so fragile.' Lean hands anchoring to her narrow wrists, he drew her to him. Slowly, sexily, he backed her down onto the opulent bed behind her. 'Then time became an issue. You deserved something more than a stolen hour. If I had been a different kind of guy, you might still have been a virgin tonight.'

'You're not that patient.'

'Would you want me to be?' He flicked loose the catch on her bra and peeled it away.

'I should say yes…' Her heart was already beating so fast with anticipation that she was breathless. 'But I'd be lying.'

As the pale voluptuous mounds of her breasts spilled free, Giannis released his breath in a deeply appreciative hiss. He bent his handsome dark head to take immediate advantage of a quivering pink peak. Supersensitive there, she whimpered and let her head fall back over his arm, her hips squirming as he teased the tender buds until each was as ripe as a berry. He pulled her on to his lap and slid his tongue into the delicate interior of her mouth, probing with erotic mastery while he played with her swollen nipples.

Faster than Maddie could have believed, she became unbearably aroused by his touch. Liquid heat coiled in her belly and set up a tingle of tormenting awareness between her slender thighs. Settling her down on the bed, he sprang upright to undress.

'*Theos mou*… I have never desired a woman as much as I desire you,' Giannis intoned. 'I didn't know I could feel like this, and every time I feel it with you I crave it again. There has been no other woman for me. Don't you ever try to disappear out of my life again.'

'Never,' she managed shakily, treasuring his every word as reassurance of the kind she most needed to feel secure.

'Or I'll tag you like a criminal…even tie you to my bed,' Giannis muttered thickly, coming down beside her again. 'But then I might never leave the bedroom, *agape mou*.'

Looking at him, she felt the inside of her mouth run dry. He was all virile male, from his strong shoulders and muscular hair-roughened chest to his long powerful thighs and aggressive arousal. He kissed her with fierce heat, and yet there was a gentle edge to his sexual urgency that filled her with delicious tension. He explored the delicate pink folds of her femininity and she shivered violently, too excited to stay still. He stroked the tiny pearl of sensitivity with a skill that made her hips writhe and her teeth clench. She was hot and swollen and damp, and the ache between her trembling thighs was edging closer and closer to pure sensual torment.

'Are you ready yet?' Giannis breathed raggedly.

'Yes…oh, yes,' she moaned.

He sank into her with a ravenous groan of raw physical pleasure, and the extreme surge of delight she experienced almost overwhelmed her. His every slow, deliberate movement electrified her. Each individual sensation was so hot and fresh and intense that her excitement kept on rising. His endurance was amazing. Tiny tremors started running riot through her. The pleasure was exquisite, making her burn and tighten and throb until at last his powerful passion pushed her to an ecstatic climax. Ripples of rapture left her ravished by the bliss of complete gratification.

Giannis tugged her down on top of him and covered her hectically flushed face with tiny featherlight kisses. The unfamiliar display of affection filled her with happiness.

She smiled giddily at him, feeling warm and loving and very lucky. 'I think you're the one who's going to end up tied to the bed,' she whispered dreamily. 'I hope it's going to be a long honeymoon.'

Giannis dealt her a lazy masculine grin. 'I think I'll be up to the challenge.'

Maddie snuggled closer. 'You didn't need to try and make me agree to marry you,' she confided. 'I hadn't the smallest intention of saying no.'

Surprise and confusion flared in his brilliant dark eyes.

Maddie grinned. 'I just thought you should know.'

The portrait of a pretty little girl with black hair and laughing brown eyes hung on the wall of Giannis's study. 'Who is she?' Maddie asked, having meant to enquire before, on another occasion, but having forgotten.

His lean strong face tensed. 'My sister, Leta.'

Maddie spun round. 'My goodness—I didn't even know you *had* a sister! I thought you were an only child.'

'People prefer to forget about Leta.' Giannis looked sombre. 'She was a passenger in the car that my father crashed on our private estate in Italy. He was drunk, and racing one of his friends for a bet. Leta was ten years old. My father walked away, but my sister suffered horrific injuries that left her disabled in mind and body. She required constant nursing care but she still recognised us...' His voice had grown rough-edged with emotion. 'I spent as much time with her as I could, but I was only thirteen and in boarding school and it was difficult.'

Warm sympathy had filled Maddie's green eyes. 'You must all have found that very difficult to deal with.'

'My parents didn't.' His lean, darkly handsome face was bleak. 'Leta was airbrushed out of our lives. They said that visiting her upset them too much. Her condition embarrassed them. When they were told that she was dying they didn't go to her, and I didn't find out until it was too late. She died alone, save for the nurses who were caring for her.'

That sad conclusion to a situation that she could tell had devastated him when he was a teenager made Maddie swallow hard. 'I'm so sorry. It would have helped you to be with her at the last.'

'Yes. But good can come out of bad. A few years afterwards Dorkas persuaded me to put my anger at Leta's lonely passing to more positive use. That was when I became involved with charities that work with terminally ill children. But I also think that's why I thought until I met you that I would never want children,' Giannis admitted. 'Maybe I was afraid that being a lousy parent was in the blood.'

'And maybe you were just remembering unhappy times and protecting yourself. That's only human,' Maddie added softly.

Giannis hovered, and then dropped a casual kiss on the top of her head. He walked out to the helicopter waiting to whisk him to Athens and then an onward flight to London. They had been together almost constantly for more than a month. About twenty feet away from the helicopter he stopped dead in his tracks, wheeled round, and strode back to her. Dark golden eyes smouldering, he closed a possessive arm to her spine to pull her close and kiss her breathless.

'What was that for?' she whispered, wide-eyed

'Don't get too used to sleeping alone in my bed, *agape mou*,' he murmured huskily.

Maddie went down to the beach accompanied by a cavalcade of willing helpers bearing a chair, a table, rugs, parasols, cool drinks and books. It was her husband's wish that she receive what she considered to be a ridiculous amount of attention. He was afraid that she might overtire herself, and he had insisted that when she was outdoors someone else should always be within reach, in case she had an accident. Getting in the water even to paddle was strictly forbidden when he was not present. She had pointed out that her gynaecologist was delighted with the way her pregnancy was progressing, but Giannis remained unconvinced.

A friend had had the poor taste to tell Giannis that twin pregnancies were more likely to end in premature labour. In an effort to educate him, and cool his apprehension on her behalf, Maddie had made the mistake of pressing a book on the subject on him. Unfortunately he had turned straight to the section on complications and discovered a bigger source of apprehension.

Maddie, however, was supremely unconcerned. She felt good. She was also feeling incredibly happy. Although she would never have risked saying it to Giannis, she believed a couple of days back at work would give his thoughts a more appropriate focus. At times he was downright exhausting to be around.

A dreamy smile softening her mouth, she sipped at her apple juice and watched the waves streaming into shore one after another, in a timeless hypnotic pattern. The constant surge of the water rolling in over the sand was as soothing to her as music. Five weeks had passed since their wedding, and even though Giannis had had to devote time to his business empire, the spirit of the honeymoon was still very much alive.

Indeed, his care and concern for her wellbeing had melted away her insecurities. He had become everything to her—a passionate lover and a fiercely entertaining, amusing companion. She loved his boundless energy and his quick, incisive mind. She had learned to appreciate his sardonic humour. In short, she absolutely adored him and could not imagine life without him.

He was teaching her Greek. She had utterly failed to teach him how to relax doing nothing. Giannis was active for eighteen hours out of every twenty-four. If she woke at dawn he was already up and about. Together they had island-hopped on the yacht, eaten in unspoilt tavernas in mountain villages and dodged photographers in more fashionable locations. They had picnicked below the plane trees his grandfather had planted at the eastern end of the island, and watched the sun go down from the little ruined temple down by the shore.

On her first night without Giannis, Maddie decided on an evening of self-indulgence. She had a bubble bath, went to bed early, ate chocolate fudge cake and tuned the television to the sort of glamorous celebrity programme that bored Giannis to death. In truth, fashion had not interested Maddie that much before her wedding, but she was planning to make more effort after the twins were born and she rediscovered her waist. Although Giannis had had an array of designer maternity clothes flown out for her benefit, Maddie remained unimpressed. All she ever saw when she looked in the mirror was the expanse of her stomach.

Feeling lazy, she was content to lie in bed and watch the famous walk up a red carpet to attend an awards ceremony. When Krista, accompanied by a minor actor, appeared in a striking silver evening gown, Maddie paid very close attention. The other woman was so extraordinarily beautiful that Maddie could never quite accept that Giannis did not suffer constant stabs of regret at having surrendered such a prize. Maddie had not told her husband about Krista's phone call on their wedding night, but she had been very relieved that it had not been repeated. On screen, the presenter approached Krista and admired her extremely elaborate diamond and sapphire necklace and drop earrings.

'They were a very special gift from Giannis Petrakos. We're still very close,' the beautiful blonde shared.

'How close is close?' the presenter joked. 'I mean, didn't Giannis Petrakos only get married last month?'

Krista laughed and widened her turquoise eyes. 'No comment. I can only tell you that I received my jewellery much more recently than that.'

After a shaken pause, Maddie hit the off button on the television remote control, and then suddenly she was scrambling in a mad rush off the bed and racing into the *en-suite* bathroom to be ingloriously sick. In the aftermath, she was shaking so badly that she had to sit down before she could gather the strength to stand up and wash. Krista's smug, self-satisfied smile kept on replaying inside her head. Could it be true? Could Giannis be seeing his former fiancée behind his wife's back?

During the past five weeks Giannis had only been absent on half a dozen occasions from her side, and not once overnight. He had gone to Athens on business. Did she believe that? He could have been meeting up with Krista somewhere. With a fleet of private jets and unlimited funds at his disposal such a liaison would be easily facilitated. Was that why she had not heard from Krista again? Had Krista been waiting for just such a moment to make her public announcement?

Maddie knew she would have no peace of mind until she had confronted Giannis. She phoned Nemos and asked him to make arrangements for her to fly to London the following morning. She told him that she intended to surprise Giannis. Even so, she thought that Giannis might ring her, because she assumed that he would soon hear about Krista's indiscreet declaration. But Giannis did not call, and Maddie got no sleep that night. She packed an overnight bag at three in the morning, tormented by questions she couldn't answer. Was her whole marriage a sham? Had he only wed her to confer legitimacy on the twin babies she carried? Or was the truth much less complex than that? Was Giannis simply a womaniser?

All of a sudden the relationship she had believed so secure seemed to be built on sand foundations. He had never promised her fidelity. He had never sworn to be with her for ever. He had never said that he loved her. But he liked her, he laughed at her jokes, he looked after her—and from the moment he woke up until the minute he finally slept at night he couldn't seem to keep his hands off her. Only that wasn't love, was it? That was good old-fashioned lust, she reminded herself unhappily.

During the flight, Maddie planned exactly what she would say. She promised herself that she would be cool and dignified while she told him that she would not live with a man who carried on with other women. Particularly Krista. Hadn't

Krista warned her that Giannis always came back to her? The
idea of Krista being with Giannis made Maddie feel hopelessly inadequate. Nothing had ever hurt her so much as the
power of her own imagination.

Nemos picked her up at the airport. 'The boss knows you're
on your way.'

Maddie was disappointed to have lost the element of
surprise. When the limo dropped her off at the City apartment,
she felt weak and shaky. But when she got into the penthouse
lift a sudden tide of rage filled her. A giant tumult of agonised
emotion was being born out of the anguish she was struggling
to contain. She stepped into the magnificent hall just as
Giannis appeared in a doorway.

'I'm really pleased that you're here, but I'm not at all
happy that you flew all this way. You must be exhausted,
pedhi mou.'

He looked breathtakingly handsome. A sleek ebony brow
quirked in a questioning move that was so familiar it hurt like
a knife twisting in her chest. All her cool and dignity died in
that moment, along with the careful script of cutting but polite
condemnation that she had planned to voice.

'You rat…I hate your guts!' Maddie launched at him, and
she yanked off her wedding ring and threw it. 'You don't appreciate me. You don't deserve me. I hope you're absolutely
miserable with Krista!'

For a split second he was stunned, and then he caught the
ring in mid-air. 'I *would* be miserable with her.'

'Then why are you having an affair with her?' Maddie sobbed.

'I swear that there is no affair—'

'I don't believe you!' Maddie dashed away the tears from
her furious eyes. 'I won't forgive you either.'

'I know you would not forgive me for infidelity, which is why you can safely believe that I will never betray you.' His dark, deep-set eyes intense, Giannis grimaced. 'I think I should have told you all this before today. But I had no idea that Krista would go to such lengths to save face.'

'Save face? What are you talking about?'

The front doorbell was buzzing.

As a manservant answered the door, Giannis took Maddie into his office and urged her to sit down. 'I believe that is Krista's father arriving. He asked if he could come to discuss what his daughter did last night. Hopefully you will find it easier to believe him.'

Her eyes widened in bewilderment. 'Her father? But what's he got to do with this?'

A portly middle-aged man with a troubled expression entered the room, and came to a surprised halt when he saw Maddie.

'Pirro Spyridou…my wife, Madeleine.'

Maddie was disconcerted when the older man immediately offered her his apologies for his daughter's comments on television the night before. 'I can't excuse her for embarrassing us all in this manner. But Krista lives for media attention, and once the engagement ended people were no longer so interested in her, which hurt her pride. She also felt that she had been made to look foolish.'

Giannis nodded acceptance of that fact.

Pirro Spyridou sighed. 'But the real problem is that she has been experimenting with drugs, and her behaviour has become more and more erratic.'

'Drugs?' Giannis ejaculated in consternation. 'Are you certain?'

'This morning Krista agreed to enter a clinic for treatment,' the older man explained heavily. 'It is not the first time she has needed help.'

'I had no idea,' Giannis admitted grimly. 'I hope that I did not contribute to the problem?'

'No. I feel that we were at fault for not warning you before the engagement.'

Equally troubled by what she was learning, Maddie described the phone call she had received from Krista on her wedding night.

Giannis frowned at Maddie. 'I wish you had shared that call and its content with me. I would've acted then, and Krista would not have made defamatory statements on television last night.' Turning back to Krista's father, he told him about the visit his daughter had made to Maddie, and Krista's proposition that she might adopt the twins and still marry Giannis.

Pirro was astonished by that story. He apologised for any distress his daughter might have caused, and began to discuss the wording of the retraction that he intended to have printed in a well-known newspaper. In that retraction, Krista's misleading statements would be withdrawn.

Giannis sighed. 'You have enough to worry about right now. Let it go, Pirro. Go home to your family. Let us forget this unpleasantness.'

The older man was embarrassingly grateful for such a level of understanding. It was clear that he was at his wits' end about how to handle his daughter's problems. With a final apology he took his leave.

'The day I finished with Krista I saw her screaming at a maid,' Giannis recalled. 'Some time afterwards I recalled that, and questioned the housekeeper about the incident. But the maid had been dismissed. Krista said she had found the maid taking drugs in her bedroom. She was probably lying. That wrong must be righted.'

'How could you have known?' Maddie was feeling distinctly shellshocked, and rather naked without the wedding ring she had thrown at Giannis. He was innocent of infidelity and blame. She had believed Krista rather than him.

'I'm sure you are wondering why I gave Krista a small fortune in diamonds. I had acquired the set as a gift for her, and I felt that she should still have it,' Giannis breathed heavily. 'I felt guilty. Neither she nor I were in love, but I should never have asked her to marry me. She got on my nerves. I was eager to be free of her. It might have been kinder if I had been more honest.'

'I don't think being told that she got on your nerves would have helped,' Maddie sighed

'But had I told her that I had fallen hopelessly in love for the first time in my life, she might at least have seen that trying to get me back was a complete waste of time.'

Maddie had a mental image of her ears perking up high like a rabbit's. 'Hopelessly in love?'

Giannis crouched down at her feet so that he could see her face. His beautiful dark eyes were usually unguarded. 'I didn't realise it until I married you. But you were never out of my mind for a moment from the first day I saw you. There has not been another woman in my arms since that day either…'

'Are you serious?' Maddie whispered, practically mesmerised by what he was telling her, and yet scared to believe in it as well.

'My desire was only for you. I couldn't control it. Yet I was still foolish to think it was just sex… I only thought in terms of sex…'

Maddie could not resist tracing the hard slant of one classic male cheekbone with a wondering forefinger. 'Oh, I know that. You were very vocal on that score. But what I don't understand is why you were ready to marry a woman you felt nothing for?'

'I had given up believing that there was a perfect woman out there for me, so when you came along I didn't recognise you.' Giannis sprang upright and shrugged. 'I was bored with dating. I didn't want to give a woman anything but money and position, and Krista was content with that. I thought it was a sensible arrangement.'

'You were lonely—'

Giannis froze. 'No, I wasn't!'

But Maddie was convinced that he had been lonely, looking for something more than casual affairs and hoping that the stability of marriage with Krista would somehow fill that lack in his life.

'I suppose I *was* lonely after you disappeared,' he ground out grudgingly. 'But that was because I'd got used to you.'

Maddie was too kind to ask him how she had contrived to become such a necessity after a mere thirty-six hours with him in Morocco.

'I should have been much more honest about Krista. I was an arrogant bastard, and I did behave badly. But when you said to me that I had been your hero as a teenager, it hurt. Those words of disappointment would not leave me alone,' Giannis admitted. 'I was ashamed, but still too stubborn to say what I should have said.'

'Why am I hearing all this now?' Maddie queried in fascination. 'You've never talked to me like this before.'

'You weren't the only person who heard Krista being interviewed on live television last night. I heard soon afterwards, and there was this deep feeling of panic, *agape mou*.' Giannis shot her a speaking appraisal. 'I knew that because I had not been more frank with you it would be very hard to convince you that Krista was lying. I was afraid that you would never believe me. When I asked myself what I would do if you walked out on me, I felt empty. I didn't know what to do. I was going to drag Pirro back to Greece with me to clear my name. I've been up all night…'

A rueful smile tugged at Maddie's tense mouth, for she could see the strain etched in his lean dark features now that she knew to look for it. 'Just like me. I couldn't bear to lose you—'

'Or I you,' Giannis confided thickly. 'What a fool I've been! All those weeks on Libos and we were so happy—and still I didn't tell you how much I cared about you, or how important you had become in my life.'

But all the time he had been *showing* her that he loved her in so many ways, Maddie reflected ruefully. Unfortunately she had been too intimidated by the spectre of Krista's apparent perfection to appreciate that Giannis was so attentive, caring, affectionate and possessive because he had fallen in love with her.

'You're telling me now. I'm better with emotions than you,' Maddie told him sunnily. 'I knew I was falling for you in Morocco—'

'But you still wouldn't have anything to do with me!' Giannis protested.

'It wouldn't have been right to do anything else when you were still engaged.'

'The only problem being that the minute I got unengaged, you vanished!' he reminded her darkly. 'I was shattered by that, and when I couldn't find you I started not sleeping.

Sometimes I'd wake up in the middle of the night and wonder if you were with some other guy. I don't ever want to live through an ordeal like that again.'

'So *behave*,' Maddie advised, relaxing enough to get cheeky. 'I can't credit that that's how you really felt. You're the man who told me that I had nothing to do with your decision to end your engagement.'

Giannis groaned at that timely reminder. 'It had *everything* to do with you, but I wasn't ready to admit that to you or myself.'

'You're so secretive,' she scolded.

'Not any more. You've got my every secret out of me,' Giannis lamented feelingly.

'It's unhealthy for you to bottle things up,' she said comfortingly. 'You've got to know I'm mad about you.'

'Barely ten minutes ago you flung your wedding ring at me!'

Maddie stuck out her finger for it to be replaced. He didn't waste any time playing hard to get on that score.

'I really, really love you,' she told him earnestly.

'Even after all that's happened?' he pressed. 'And everything that's gone wrong?'

Maddie pretended to think about that question, for her confidence was growing by leaps and bounds and she decided to tease him. 'Well, there were times when I was worried it might just be sex…'

Giannis leapt upright and bent down to scoop her up like a parcel from the sofa. 'We'll go to bed and find out, shall we?'

'Is that your answer to everything?' Maddie giggled, thinking that they were wonderfully well matched in that department.

'When you're in my arms in bed you feel one hundred per cent mine. It feels amazingly good,' Giannis confided, and he kissed her long, slow and deep, until her toes curled inside her shoes.

She wrapped her arms round his neck. 'Hmm…'

'I'm never going to let you go, *agape mou*,' he swore, with satisfying fervour.

Almost eighteen months later, Maddie watched her children toddle about below the shaded loggia on the roof terrace of their Moroccan home. Her son, Rodas, had black curly hair and enormous energy. Always exploring, he needed careful supervision, and plenty to keep him occupied. Her daughter, Suzy, was as copper-haired as her mother and was as calm as her brother was over-active. A tolerant baby, she slept when she was expected to sleep, and played in an orderly manner. Maddie was grateful she had a nanny to give her a break when she needed one, or wanted to spend time alone with Giannis.

Giannis adored his children. From the instant the twins had arrived in the world, with remarkably little fuss, Giannis had been a devoted father. Some of their most happy moments had been family ones, when they'd fooled around with the twins, or paused to marvel at a first word or step. Time and love had given Maddie a lot more confidence in herself and in her marriage.

Krista had been through rehab and had recently married a Hollywood movie mogul twice her age. She was regularly featured in glossy magazines, wearing the latest fashion and arriving at the most exclusive events. She seemed happy, which pleased Maddie, who sometimes felt a little guilty about the extent of her own blissful contentment.

Giannis had been nagged out of being a workaholic. When he had discovered that babies had bodyclocks that disliked changing time-zones he'd begun to travel a lot less. Also, he disliked being away from his family for longer than a couple of days. They spent a great deal of time on the island of Libos, where Dorkas was a regular visitor to their home. Once the children reached school age, however, Giannis and Maddie were planning on settling at Harriston Hall during the week, for Maddie wanted them to enjoy an English education. Here, at the old fortress in the High Atlas Mountains of Morocco, was where they always came to relax and take advantage of just being with each other.

With the help of the children's nanny Maddie put the twins to bed for the night. That afternoon she had had a massage and beauty session. Now she shed her casual clothing and dressed to impress in a flimsy lingerie set, followed by an azure-blue cocktail dress and high heels. Smoothing the stretchy fabric over her hips, she smiled when she heard the helicopter coming in to land. It had taken hard work and will-power, and a personal trainer, but she had regained her waist. When Giannis walked in she was posed by the terrace doors.

'I have died and gone to heaven,' Giannis murmured, his deeply appreciative gaze locked to his red-headed temptress of a wife. 'You look fit to ravish.'

'You didn't spend long with the twins.'

'For once in their lives they're both fast asleep on schedule,' he told her huskily. 'And, wonderful though my son and daughter are, it's been three long days since I saw my wife.'

'You've been counting?'

Giannis curved an admiring hand to the full curve of her derrière and eased her up against his lithe, powerful frame. For a moment he just held her close, with the affection that was becoming more and more natural to him. When he lifted his handsome dark head again, his dark golden eyes smouldered with possessive heat over her lovely face. 'When I'm away I miss you. You've changed my life around, *agape mou*.'

'And there's me thinking I was being so subtle,' Maddie teased, leaning into him with alacrity, loving the familiar feel and warmth of him.

Giannis set her back from him and lifted her wrist to clasp around it a shimmering diamond bracelet adorned with the letter M. 'Happy birthday.'

'It's gorgeous.'

'Like that outfit,' Giannis remarked huskily, stepping back from the temptation of getting too close to her shapely body. 'Hamid is waiting to serve a very fancy meal in honour of your special day.'

Maddie stretched up to kiss him, and that one taste led to another taste, and then she started wrenching at his tie—until she too remembered the birthday meal, and strove to behave with greater self-discipline.

'I love you very much, Mrs Petrakos,' Giannis murmured over the exquisitely presented dinner. 'How am I doing in the hero stakes?'

'You'll have to show me,' Maddie whispered, her attention glued to his lean, dark face with sensual intent.

'So you work on a basis of continual assessment?' Giannis drawled with a wicked grin.

Mid-meal, the long, languishing looks, the flirtation and the ever-increasing urge to touch triumphed, and they vanished into the bedroom. Giannis kissed her breathless and told her that she was the most irresistible woman alive. Maddie thought about how much she adored him, and decided that exercise would do her much more good than dessert.

HARLEQUIN®

Mediterranean NIGHTS™

Experience glamour, elegance, mystery and revenge aboard the high seas....

Coming in September 2007...

BREAKING ALL THE RULES

by

Marisa Carroll

Aboard the cruise ship *Alexandra's Dream* for some R & R, sports journalist Lola Sandler is surprised to spot pro-golfer Eric Lashman. Years after walking away from the pro circuit with no explanation to the public, Eric now finds himself teaching aboard a cruise ship.

Lola smells a career-making exposé... but their developing relationship may force her to make a difficult choice.

HM38963

REQUEST YOUR FREE BOOKS!

2 FREE NOVELS PLUS 2 FREE GIFTS!

YES! Please send me 2 FREE Harlequin Presents® novels and my 2 FREE gifts. After receiving them, if I don't wish to receive any more books, I can return the shipping statement marked "cancel." If I don't cancel, I will receive 6 brand-new novels every month and be billed just $3.80 per book in the U.S., or $4.47 per book in Canada, plus 25¢ shipping and handling per book and applicable taxes, if any*. That's a savings of close to 15% off the cover price! I understand that accepting the 2 free books and gifts places me under no obligation to buy anything. I can always return a shipment and cancel at any time. Even if I never buy another book from Harlequin, the two free books and gifts are mine to keep forever.

106 HDN EEXK 306 HDN EEXV

Name	(PLEASE PRINT)

Address		Apt. #

City	State/Prov.	Zip/Postal Code

Signature (if under 18, a parent or guardian must sign)

Mail to the **Harlequin Reader Service®**:
IN U.S.A.: P.O. Box 1867, Buffalo, NY 14240-1867
IN CANADA: P.O. Box 609, Fort Erie, Ontario L2A 5X3

Not valid to current Harlequin Presents subscribers.

Want to try two free books from another line?
Call 1-800-873-8635 or visit www.morefreebooks.com.

* Terms and prices subject to change without notice. NY residents add applicable sales tax. Canadian residents will be charged applicable provincial taxes and GST. This offer is limited to one order per household. All orders subject to approval. Credit or debit balances in a customer's account(s) may be offset by any other outstanding balance owed by or to the customer. Please allow 4 to 6 weeks for delivery.

Your Privacy: Harlequin is committed to protecting your privacy. Our Privacy Policy is available online at www.eHarlequin.com or upon request from the Reader Service. From time to time we make our lists of customers available to reputable firms who may have a product or service of interest to you. If you would prefer we not share your name and address, please check here. ☐

HP07

The big miniseries from

HARLEQUIN *Presents*

Bedded by *Blackmail*

Forced to bed...then to wed?

Dare you read it?

He's got her firmly in his sights
and she has only one chance
of survival—surrender to his
blackmail...and him...in his bed!

September's arrival:

BLACKMAILED INTO
THE ITALIAN'S BED
by Miranda Lee

Jordan had struggled to forget Gino Bortelli,
but suddenly the arrogant, sexy Italian was back,
and he was determined to have Jordan in his bed again....

Coming in October:

WILLINGLY BEDDED,
FORCIBLY WEDDED
by Melanie Milburne
Book #2673